ENDO

BLAIR'S GAP

Blair's Gap is a dramatic tale of an individual journey to Christ that can only be described as a Saul to Paul experience. The battle for our individual souls is real. *Blair's Gap* keeps your interest from beginning to conclusion. I just could not stop reading as I was curious as to what the ending would be. I knew that the author was still among us, so I assumed that everything would turn out, but how was the question. Before the light there was darkness. The reader is propelled into the dark realm of "evil." Parts of the story are tense and frightening and Stephen-King-like. Finally, the reader learns that the light is always the brightest in the darkest room. *Blair's Gap* is a powerful and hopeful story that is supported by Scripture.

— Bruce Elliott
RN, MS, Retired VA Nurse

If you have any doubts to the existence of dark influences or that there is a way to find victory over them, *Blair's Gap* is the book for you. "Ye are of God, little children, and have overcome them: because greater is he that is in you, than he that is in the world" (1 John 4:4). *Blair's Gap* is a courageous and candid account of one man's battle and confrontation with the reality that mortal man is not here alone on this earth. David's personal life story reveals the realities of a ruthless and dark presence. More importantly, David's journey exemplifies a triumphant escape from an invisible bondage.

— Doug Evans,
Senior Pastor, First Baptist Church,
Wyoming, NY

Blair's Gap was riveting. As I wandered down the path with the main character (David) and back, I found myself being David many times as I saw my own path and the many times I headed down the wrong one, the many times tragedy was averted and the evil one was cast off. I was caught in the suspense but also relieved as the story continued always heading toward the light. David's story shows all of us that with God's strength and our own tenacity we can and will find the right path.

— Kevin Palmiter,
Pastor, Little Genesee Seventh Day Baptist Church,
Little Genesee, NY

Blair's Gap will do more than hold your interest! It'll grab you and hold you by your heart! With each successive chapter having more suspense than the previous, the author beautifully, almost poetically, describes in living color what it was like to find what he'd been looking for all along, relationship with the Son of the living God, Jesus Christ. I was blown away! David really hit it out of the park. I'm buying a dozen copies once this book comes off the press!

— Dan Woodard
Director of Leadership Development,
Inter-Act Ministries of Canada

BLAIR'S GAP

Silencing a Multi-Generational Curse

DAVID V. BURDICK

Deep River Books

Blair's Gap: Silencing a Multi-Generational Curse

Published by Deep River Books
Sisters, Oregon
www.deepriverbooks.com

Scriptures are from The Holy Bible, King James Version. Cambridge Edition: 1769 (public domain).

ISBN – 13: 9781632694454
Library of Congress: 2017943598

Printed in the USA
Cover design by Jason Enterline

Author's Website: www.firstvespers.com

TABLE OF CONTENTS

FOREWORD

In the grand scheme of our North American culture, David and I were both raised breathing secular humanistic air. David's family was Catholic; I would refer to my family as dutifully Baptist. Both of us were religious, but with the passing of each year after 1963 when the US Supreme Court declared public school-sponsored Bible reading in the United States to be unconstitutional, our culture (and subsequently our education) steadily became influenced by secularism.

Three millennia ago a wise king offered us a different perspective when he wrote that God has set eternity in the human heart, suggesting that each one of us lives with a God-shaped vacuum. Secularism (and religion in general, for that matter) tends to leave its followers with a feeling of "there must be more to life than this." The past half century offers no lack of examples of our culture's quest to fill this vacuum. In David's case his intrigue and quest for the spiritual in some ways began with the family Ouija board and séances and led to other doorways of the spirit world. Indeed, our God-shaped vacuum was designed to compel us to look for Him, but it's easy to become sidetracked.

My own introduction to the spirit world came very early in my ministry in Canada in the winter of 1979. I was pastoring a Native Indian church in northern Manitoba in fifty-below temperatures. In the community where I served, the Christ-followers explained to me that in the dead of winter when there's eighteen to nineteen hours of darkness combined with much alcohol and poker, it's quite common for spirit beings to be seen wandering around in the bush, sometimes holding candles. The community residents commonly understood that these beings should never be approached because they were evil and the source of much fear. People who didn't understand the power of the Holy Spirit would be extremely frightened of these manifestations. I have given my life to serving alongside Native pastors and encouraging them in the helping of others to find freedom from their bondage, addictions, and fears.

Over five decades of memories returned as I read through *Blair's Gap: Silencing a Multi-Generational Curse*. David's narrative of his journey is very descriptive, very real, and very readable. *Blair's Gap* will do more than hold your interest! It'll grab you and hold you by your heart! As I made my way through David's riveting story of his search for reality, I found myself walking the journey with him. I was in tears a few times and pretty scared a couple of other times. David's story is powerful because it documents a journey of epic fear and bondage that results in freedom, understanding, acceptance, and love. You will likely find yourself identifying with either himself or someone in his family. His family's dynamics may in some ways remind you of your family dynamics. With each successive chapter having more suspense than the previous, David beautifully, almost poetically, describes in living color what it was like to search for and find what he'd been looking for all along . . . relationship with the only One who delivers us from all our fears and truly satisfies the deepest longings of our soul . . . the Son of the living God, Jesus Christ. I was blown away!! David really hit it out of the park.

Rev. Dan Woodard
Native Church Consultant
Director of Leadership Development
InterAct Ministries of Canada
Carstairs, Alberta

ACKNOWLEDGMENTS

I am eternally grateful to our God who is with me always and makes all things possible. You are unconditional love, forgiveness without measure, and worthy of all praise. You are my purpose, my meaning, and my direction. I am your portion, and you are my prize.

I thank my wife who has stood by me through two books and thirty-plus years of marriage despite me. She is a strong woman who has overcome much adversity and is loved by many. I am truly blessed to have such a beautiful and supportive partner in this journey we call our lives.

Special thanks to my sister. My story couldn't have been told without sharing a very personal and private portion of her story. Thank you for making this book possible, sharing your memories, your vulnerabilities, and your countless reviews and grammatical corrections.

Lastly, I need to thank all the characters who are called out by name in my story. They have read what I have written about them and despite possibly infringing on their privacy and personal embarrassment, support my story and gave me permission to publish their names.

1

BLAIR'S GAP

Point of Awareness

"Oh, mighty and powerful God who art with me always, my right arm and my strength, so much easier is it to give you thanks when I have my daily bread and a promise of tomorrow than when my life is in turmoil and my faith is tested. So often, my God, I stand alone. So often I am broken. Where is my helper, my God, if not in you? I am sucked down to the depths of sorrow and despair. I am absent all love but yours. Pick me up once more I pray and will my legs to move. Take from me my destroying pride and self-pity. Pick me up once more I pray and give me strength to move."

I find myself at what appears to be a familiar fork in the road, a choice of direction that seems both familiar and somehow different. The path to the left is worn, well-traveled, and free of obvious obstructions. The path to the right is not so worn; it runs along a narrow ridge and is obstructed every few feet by briers and overgrown bushes. How did I get here? How long have I been sitting here? I've lost track. Has it been minutes, hours, or days?

As I look for something I might recognize, something to jar my memory, I spin my head and look behind me to find that I am, in fact, not at a fork in the road, but rather, I am at a crossing between two paths, a well-traveled path to my left and a narrow, less-traveled path to my right. How did I get here? Which path had I taken to get here and why had I come? I didn't know.

That was when I noticed the scratches on my arms. Perhaps I had walked the narrow path, and the scratches on my arms were from the briers and overgrown bushes. I didn't know. My pants were free of tears, and my sneakers appeared free of dirt. For whatever reason, I decided to backtrack just a bit down the narrow path to my right as I stood and turned back around, while I still knew which paths were coming and which were going. Perhaps that would stir my memory and help me to recall how I had arrived here.

I was only a few feet down the path when I began to remember things, unrelated things that seemed not to make much sense at the time. The last thing I remembered, or the first thing I remembered, I am not sure how to define it, was that my cousin Bruce was in the process of writing some music for me. As I walked further down the path, I wondered why my cousin was composing music for me. Then I remembered that I was intending to release three video poems that I had prepared PowerPoint presentations for. Why had I prepared PowerPoint presentations? I took another step. Oh yeah, my friend Pastor Craig planned to read the poems aloud while my cousin's music played in the background, and my friend Kent would video record the entire process for each poem. That was how it worked. Each memory triggered more questions, and the farther I traveled back down the path, the more I remembered.

The poems were an excerpt from a book I had written over the course of the last five years. The book, *First Vespers—Spiritual Verses of Hope and Inspiration*, was just published in 2014.

The videos would be an attempt to share what I had learned of Christ on my journey and perhaps promote some additional book sales.

I looked back to see if I could still see the intersection of paths that I had come from. I could just barely see the crossing. Behind me, the path was long and narrow, just as it was in front of me. I saw a small clearing where the wider path crossed the narrow path. I decided to press on just a little bit further, until it all made sense. As I turned back around, I heard the faint sound of running water. I ventured forward for another fifty or sixty feet. Pushing bushes and branches aside, I came upon a five-foot-wide, fast-running stream—the source of the water I had heard.

The stream looked clear and cold, maybe just a foot or so deep. I rolled up my pant legs and took my sneakers and socks off. Although I could probably have easily tossed my shoes across the narrow brook, I held them in my hand as I waded across. By then, I remembered why I wrote the book. I remembered when the Holy Spirit of God first spoke to me and I recognized His voice. "This is your time on the mountain. Use it wisely."

I knew in that instant that my time away from my wife and family was intended to serve God. What I didn't know was how I would go about doing it. As I recounted the few things in life that I had been good at, I remembered that I had been recognized for my poetry in college. I had been published in six consecutive semi-annual issues of the American Collegiate Poets Anthology between 1981 and 1983.

I decided to try my hand at Christian poetry. I studied the crucifixion and wrote my first poem, "Imagine Knowing." The poem was unlike any that I had previously written in that the thought of my Lord crawling brought me to tears. I e-mailed it to a Christian friend and said a prayer: "God, if this is how I will serve you, give me a sign that I will know it."

Two hours later, I received an e-mail from a pastor in a church that I had never heard of. It was a request to use the poem I had just written in an upcoming joint Good Friday Service with the participation of multiple congregations and clergy friends. That was my sign. My friend Kent had shared the poem with Pastor Craig, a man I did not know at the time, but today is a dear friend of mine. Soon I had a request for another poem. Kent and Craig became the reviewers and biblical fact-checkers of my work. One poem led to another, and five years later, I had an entire book of Christian poetry.

Just beyond the stream, the narrow path rose up and over a steep, overgrown bank. I decided I would climb to the top of the small bank to see what I could see, to remember what I could remember. At the bottom of the bank, I remembered my prayer. I had been unemployed for over two years, my wife and I had spent our entire savings trying to survive, we were down to our last $800, and we had no way to make our mortgage payment.

When my wife left that morning, I fell to my knees in tears, praying, "Dear God, have I not done what you have asked of me? Have I not been faithful? My wife can no longer bear this burden. Please God, help me! In Jesus name, I pray. Amen." Ten minutes later, the phone rang and I had an offer for the highest paying and best job of my life. Within a few days, I drove to Wisconsin to start that job, and within a few weeks, I was writing my first devotional work *First Vespers—Spiritual Verses of Hope and Inspiration.*

When the book was finally complete, I submitted my manuscript to the first reputable publisher I could find. Within a few weeks, the publisher contacted me to let me know he liked my book, but his publishing company would be contractually unable to do anything with it because they now worked exclusively for ancient alien theorists. He asked if he could forward my manuscript to some of his former employees that had formed their own publishing company. I, of course, agreed.

A few weeks later, I heard from the second publisher. The head of the publishing company said she liked the book, but she would have a hard time getting behind it because she was a devout Scientologist. She said she knew a lot of people in Christian publishing circles and asked if she could forward my manuscript to another publishing company. Again, I agreed.

The third publisher turned out to be one of the nation's leading Christian publishers, Deep River Books of Sisters, Oregon, and within two weeks they picked up my book.

Paying closer attention to my step, I reached for a branch with my right hand and placed my left foot against the base of a sapling to work my way to the top of the small bank. Sadness overtook me. When I reached the top of the bank, I could see down the other side. Another well-traveled and wider path again crossed the narrow path I was on. I walked down the far side of the small hill toward the second crossing. I was weeping and smiling at the same time. I received my first shipment of promotional books on a Thursday and coincidently had already made arrangements to meet a lady after church that Sunday to hear her testimony for another project I was working on. I decided to give her a copy of *First Vespers*. As it turned out, she was a youth minister at the First Baptist Church on Oak Island, and her students were studying the armor of Christ, the subject of my poem "Psalm 151." That very night, Cindy recited my poem to her youth group. The first book out of the box was serving God's purpose on the first day it saw light. *First*

Vespers—Spiritual Verses of Hope and Inspiration was officially released on April 10, 2014. Within two weeks, I was selected as Deep River's Author of the Month and Amazon.com temporarily sold out of books.

It occurred to me I might never find my way out of the woods. I didn't want to backtrack any further down the narrow path, past the second intersection of paths, for fear of getting lost, so I climbed back to the top of the small hill I had just descended. With no logical thought of why I did it, I tore off my T-shirt sleeve and tied it to a bush at the top of the hill before I headed back to the intersection where I had first found myself lost. It was effortless re-tracking my steps this time, and I easily found my way back to the first intersection of paths in less than an hour.

I tried to remain calm and think through my journey. To retrace the wide and well-traveled path, I would need to take the path to my right as I returned to the intersection of the two paths. To continue on, I could take the narrow path directly across the intersection, or I could take the wide and more traveled path to my left. Although it seemed obvious by now I had previously been down the narrow path I had just retraced, I chose to follow the wide and more traveled path to my right.

At first, I remembered the lies, then the drug abuse, and then the loveless sex. It all came flooding back. There were no obstructions in the wide and well-traveled path. I walked down the path quickly. I recalled the deep hatred, every deceitful act, the self-loathing, and the petty jealousies. My memories were dirty and ugly. I hurried down the path, not wanting to linger.

Eventually, I again reached a narrow stream. This time, there were six large, staggered, and evenly spaced rocks set in the streambed, obviously used as stepping stones to cross the creek. Directly opposite the stream was a small hill, having ten or fifteen stone steps. By the time I reached the top, I remembered my mother's table; Alfreido; the recollection; the appointment; the Black Forest, and the man in the mirror. At the top of the hill I discovered stone steps going down the far side.

Not surprisingly, forty or fifty feet past the bottom of the steps, I saw a narrow path that crossed the wide path I was on. Using the stone steps now as a clear landmark, I felt comfortable heading toward the intersection of the two paths without getting further lost. I walked down the hill, put the stone steps to my back, and proceeded to the intersection.

Standing at the crossing, my mind drifted to obscure thoughts of broken promises I had long since buried and forgotten. Considering everything else going on, this didn't seem at all that strange to me at the time. Possible similarities between the broken promises and the crossing paths went unnoticed.

My thoughts drifted to forty years earlier when I was stationed with the Navy on the aircraft carrier the USS Oriskany. I was in a small, elite group of the Weapons Department known as the Special Weapons Unit. Only the ship's captain, the gunner, a chief, and a small crew of maybe ten bomb technicians were allowed to enter the shop and magazines. I worked in probably the most secure location on the entire ship. Access points required several picture IDs and were guarded by armed Marines in cages. The shop area consisted of a couple of offices, a small lounge, and a locker room. It seemed the perfect place to hide something you never wanted to be found.

One day I called a friend and coworker over to my locker. He was on temporary assignment and working nights as a master-at-arms, military police investigator. John and I had been friends for a long time, and we often joined forces to explore foreign ports and party. It's hard to say, but John had probably carried me back to the boat more times than I did him.

I trusted him implicitly, and we are friends to this day. Not working together and infrequently seeing each other at the time, I showed John a small bag of marijuana that I had hidden in my inspection gloves in the top drawer of my locker, plus a few pre-rolled marijuana joints that I had hidden in the bottom of a soft pack of long cigarettes, in the bottom drawer. I gave John my combination and told him to feel free to help himself if he wanted to smoke a joint some night.

The very next morning, the gunner announced at muster that the entire ship was having locker inspections that morning to search for drugs. The gunner said he knew he had nothing to worry about, but he had instructed the chief to conduct the search anyway just to reassure the captain. John was there when the gunner made his announcement. He said he could physically see the color leaving my body. I held a final top secret clearance, and I knew at that point my career was over. I would be in the brig by that afternoon and flown out to Leavenworth Prison within a week. I vowed to keep my mouth shut and quietly prayed like I had never prayed before. "God, just give me one more chance. I will change my ways; I swear I will. Please just give me one more chance, God."

We all unlocked our lockers and waited for the chief to inspect them, one at a time. I sat on a table about ten feet directly across from the front of my open locker. I had plenty of time to pray more. "God, I promise to clean up my act and never do drugs again."

After the longest fifteen minutes of my life, the chief finally made it to my locker. He opened my top drawer, grabbed my inspection gloves with his left hand, and held them near his left shoulder to keep them from getting dirty while he rifled through the remaining contents of the drawer with his right hand. I could see the bag of marijuana inside the gloves from where I sat. When the chief had finished, he put the gloves back in the drawer, closed it, and opened the bottom drawer for inspection. The chief ran his hands through everything, picked up the soft pack of long cigarettes, swiped them under his nose, said, "smells like marijuana," laughed, threw them back in the drawer, and moved on to the next locker. I had had some close calls before, but none like that. All the promises I had made to God that day were broken later that night.

I looked up the narrow path to my right and saw it—my T-shirt sleeve tied to a small bush at the top of the hill. It was then I realized how I had gotten there. The narrow path and the wide path had been intertwined, and I had taken them both to wind up at the intersection where I began this day.

Playing it safe, I made my way back up the stone steps and took the well-traveled and quicker path back to the intersection where I had started. The entire walk back, I wondered about the why. I now knew the "how" of how I wound up where I was; what I didn't know was the "why," and more importantly, "why now?" As I approached the intersection where my day began, I understood. I had been here before. I was broken and alone. I was at God's mercy. What would I do differently? I didn't know.

I sat on the ground at that intersection of the four paths for a long time, deciding which way I should go, recalling what I had seen on the narrow path I had retraced that morning and the wide path I had just returned from. Somehow, I knew the paths would never cross again and God had called me to make a decision. Now I knew. I had to go one way or the other, but I could no longer walk blindly down whichever path I chose without considering the consequences.

My thoughts went to the narrow path I had taken that morning. I thought of Mike and Carl. Mike was replacing a worn throttle cable on my motorcycle. He was a new Christian, young in his walk, and fascinated with my book. Mike introduced me to the world of Christian Biker Clubs and convinced me I should write a book of Christian biker testimonies—Hell's Angels, Pagans, and Mongols who had turned their lives around; good men and women who had lived the life and seen some things; people who by the grace of God had found Jesus and changed the course of their lives; people who had crossed the great abyss; modern-day motorcycle apostles who had a road to Damascus experience and were willing to share their story for the greater good of spreading the word. I agreed after I met Carl and determined to call my book *Christian Soldiers on Iron Horses*.

Carl had been in the shop earlier that day looking over a set of used handlebars. For some reason, he decided to come back just as I gave Mike a pile of flyers to see if I could solicit testimonies for the "Christian Soldiers" project. As I told Mike a bit of my testimony and we talked about the plan, Carl listened intently. I assumed he was waiting to make Mike an offer for the handlebars he was again holding. To my surprise, when there was a break in the conversation, Carl began sharing his testimony.

As it turned out, Carl and I had much in common; we had been down many of the same paths in life and wound up in much the same place. We worked at carnivals in our youth, had trouble finding our way in life, abused whatever drugs were available, loved riding motorcycles, eventually sobered up, and found Christ by the grace of God. Now we were taking part in the Great Commission and sharing our testimony with whomever would listen.

About ten minutes later, I stopped Carl in the middle of his testimony and asked him if I could interview him with my recorder for use in the "Christian Soldiers" project. He agreed, but told me he had been down in North Carolina on vacation and would be returning home to Tennessee the following afternoon. Carl then gave me his address in Ocean City, and I agreed to drive down to meet him there early the next morning. Typical of me, I got lost just a few blocks from Carl's apartment and had to call him for additional directions. When Carl figured out where I was, he and his wife drove out to meet me, and I followed them back to their apartment. After introductions, Carl's wife left us alone, and Carl shared his testimony with me over the course of the next three hours.

His testimony began as a carnival worker and intravenous heroin addict who had just quit his job and was hitchhiking across the lower United States to find his brother. I identified with his story. I too had worked for a traveling carnival and hitchhiked everywhere when I was sixteen. Carl touched briefly on his time spent as a prison chaplain and finished his story with his work as a Christian missionary in Rwanda, unable to speak the language, but leading a Rwandan woman to Christ.

Carl shared with me a vision he had experienced one day while praying to see God. Christ was holding his face in the palms of His hands, touching His forehead to Carl's forehead, and locking eyes with him. Carl was filled with a deep and sincere love he had not previously known and Christ asked, "Is that good enough?" Carl and I both wept as he told me of his vision. I knew from my own experience that he had experienced the presence of God and was telling me the truth.

As the sun retreated, the woods were getting a little dimmer. I could still easily see and pick out the leaves and branches against the sky; however, the colors of the leaves and grasses at ground level were now shades of gray. Rather than continuing my journey and leaving as I probably should have, my thoughts shifted to the wider path I had last taken.

I remembered the fifteen-year-old girl in the Philippines. I had been drinking gin all day. The country was under martial law, and everyone had to be off the streets by midnight. I was heading back to the base at a quarter to twelve and all the prostitutes that hadn't found a customer from one of the bars that evening were now looking to capture a sailor on his way home. I said, "No, thank you" to many ladies by the time the girl grabbed my arm. Though I can make no excuse for myself, she was cute as a button and I was only seventeen. She grabbed my arm and wasn't about to let go. I said, "No, thank you" several times, but she refused to let go of my arm and followed me for three blocks. Finally, I said, "I've been drinking all day. I am drunk, and I only have a dollar left in my wallet." Her reply was, "I'll take you home for a dollar." A decent man would have given her the dollar at that point and walked the last two blocks to the base. Instead, I said, "Okay," and I went home with her.

I don't remember her name and that was the only night I ever saw her. She took me to an area known as shantytown, the poorest area in the entire city of Olongapo, a place I never would have dared walk during the light of day. It was an area just behind the main strip of bars and was cluttered with hundreds of bamboo huts, ten or fifteen feet apart, and none with plumbing or running water. As shanties go, hers was a nice one. We entered by a hallway where her father slept in a hammock suspended along a shared wall with the one bedroom. I was surprised to see what appeared to be a very nice queen-sized bed standing on the dirt floor. From the look of the neighborhood, I assumed everyone would be sleeping on mats. The girl sat me on the foot of the bed where I leaned over and began to untie my shoes. When I sat back up, she pushed me back on the bed and took my shoes off. We exchanged pleasantries, and I gave her the single dollar in my wallet with no remorse.

At the time, this was nothing more than a great Navy story about how I slept with an entire family for a dollar. Twenty years later, I understood the level of poverty, love, and sadness that would have to exist to allow a father to overlook so much to feed his family a single cup of white rice the next day. I was so ashamed of myself. I could not sleep with this shameful sin any longer, so I sponsored a four-year-old girl on the island of Mindanao. My wife and I sponsored that same girl for nearly three years until the girl's family was sufficiently well off that she could no longer qualify for the program.

The sun now hovered on the horizon, and the sky was turning dark. I needed to get moving soon. I had no means to start a fire, and if I didn't find my way quickly, I would have to spend the night alone in the dark, somewhere in an unknown forest. My first thought was to take the unexplored, but well-traveled path that would certainly be the faster of the two and the easiest to follow. That was when it all began to make sense. I had been walking aimlessly my entire life. I had gone where I chose and when I chose. I had been chasing pipedreams and momentary worldly desires. My life had no purpose or direction. By the grace of God, I had occasionally stumbled across the narrow path that leads to the eye of the needle. I had stumbled across the narrow path enough that I could now recognize it.

Mark 12:25 came to mind: "*It is easier for a camel to go through the eye of a needle, than for a rich man to enter into the kingdom of God.*" I had studied theology enough to know that the "eye of a needle" was a low, arched passageway designed to keep camels from entering a courtyard. While in no way an easy accomplishment, a camel can go through the eye of a needle if lying down and dragged through on a mat.

I recalled Scriptures I had learned in my research for writing *First Vespers*. Proverbs 14:15–16, 18, says, "*The simple believeth every word: but the prudent man looks well to his going. A wise man fears, and departs from evil: but the fool rages, and is confident. The simple inherit folly: but the prudent are crowned with knowledge.*" Suddenly, the Scriptures I recalled came to life. I was at the straight gate that leads to the narrow way and the wide gate that leads to the broad way. I stood where the paths crossed—the point of awareness. I remembered Matthew 7:13–14, which says, "*Enter ye in at the straight gate: for wide is the gate, and broad is the way that leads to destruction, and many there be which go in there at: Because straight is the gate, and narrow is the way, which leads unto life; and few there be that find it.*" Facing the paths I had not yet traveled—the long and narrow path to my right and the wide and well-traveled path to my left—I took the narrow path to my right.

At first, everything was black; the path was narrow and not well-defined. I struggled to ensure I was still on the path and not just walking aimlessly in the woods. Within an hour, my eyes finally adjusted, and I could see the stars that filled the sky. The moon shown directly over the narrow path in the direction I headed. I was aware the light pollution of the earth tends to dull out the stars of the sky. By the brilliance and great quantity of stars in the sky, I knew I was nowhere near a city or well-populated area. Perhaps because I was so preoccupied with not getting lost, memories of the wide path faded away.

Within another hour, the tops of the trees were thinning out. I could see more sky and fewer branches. Thirsty, I hoped I would find another stream as I approached the edge of the woods or a clearing. I pushed on. Sure enough, within fifteen minutes I walked out into a great meadow of grasses. The grasses were bent over, blowing in a gentle, warm evening breeze, brightly lit by the moon.

My mind was suddenly at ease and clear. It all made sense. I thought of Blair's Gap and the man in the mirror. My great-grandfather, perhaps my grandfather, my father, and I had all been to Blair's Gap. For my great-grandfather, it was the overwhelming temptation of one of three chests at a campsite in the woods; for my father, it was the life and death choices made in one of four cellblocks at Attica; and for me, it was the temporary satisfaction of worldly self-indulgence and the ease of obtaining it on one of two paths in a dark forest.

"Holy Father in heaven who art with me always, give me remembrance of your good graces that I may find the wisdom to always be humble. Grant me remembrance of your great mercies that I may always be thankful. Allow me remembrance of your mighty hand and let me contemplate your absence that I may learn to be fearful. God, build my faith through gentle correction and answer to prayer. In Jesus' great name I pray, Amen."

The recurring nightmares are now gone, and the echoes of my mother's table, Alfreido, and Blair's Gap can barely be heard. For a fraction of a second, I wondered if I had made the right choice, if I had taken the right path. Then I knew I had. I only walked in the meadow a short time before I became aware I had been stumbling in a dark forest for many years. Without further thought, I lay down in the tall grasses to rest and see what tomorrow would bring.

Unlike the day before, whatever gifts or challenges tomorrow would bring would no longer be up to me. I will follow the narrow path, clear the briers as I go, and search out the narrow gate until this life is over. For me, there is no other choice. I've seen the meadow.

In the end, I found the living God in whom all things are possible, the God who answers my prayers and whose blessings are tangible because Jesus told me that I could and I believed Him. I found the door by which any man may enter to be saved, the door that leads to the pasture where I rest my head and set my burdens down (John 10:9). Psalm 36:7–8 says, "*How excellent is thy loving kindness, O God! I put my trust in the shadow of your wings. I am abundantly satisfied with the fatness of your house. I drink of the river of your pleasures.*"

I have found you, Lord, my purpose, my meaning, and my direction. I am your portion, and you are my prize. You are unconditional love, forgiveness without measure, and worthy of all praise. Without you, my God, I have only momentary pleasures and fleeting desires of a worldly path to destruction. You are everything that is good. I cannot possibly return the love you have shown me, but I will try. All that I have is yours.

2

THE RECOLLECTION

The Devil's Fire

By all accounts, my childhood was not usual. By my fifteenth birthday, I had seen and experienced things that others would never see or experience, nor would they want to. I wasn't aware of it at the time, but a hook had been ever so gingerly set. I was being reeled in a little bit at a time, always drawing ever closer to the boat and the darkness of this world and captivity. The same hook had been set with my great-grandfather three generations earlier. I was in for the long pull.

I knew nothing of the recollection when I stepped out of the bathtub that night in Ohio, wiped off the mirror, and saw the traveler sitting on the washing machine behind me. I had no idea of who the traveler was or how the traveler, the recollection, my mother's table, and a stone icon would all come together to form the story of Blair's Gap. Nor did I foresee how Blair's Gap would inevitably taunt me for nearly a quarter of my life.

I first heard of the recollection in the summer of 1971, shortly after my mother held a séance in Columbus, Ohio, where my father was invited to meet with the traveler at Blair's Gap. My father's mother, my grandmother Nora, told me of the recollection when I returned home. Years later, after much pestering, she wrote down what she could remember, answered questions, and filled in whatever details she could.

Around the turn of the twentieth century, Nora's father Clifton, my great-grandfather, worked the Western Pennsylvania gas lines for a Guitonville-based enterprise known as United Natural Gas. Teams of horses were driven to accomplish most of the work required to install and maintain the wells. Despite the largest portion of the work taking place in the gas and oil fields, my great-grandfather was known to have walked his fair share of lines. Lines were checked for leaks and fires. Thunderstorms were common in the summer and lightning was responsible for many forest fires. By 1910, Great-grandfather was promoted to foreman and bookkeeper of United Natural Gas and moved from Queen to Guitonville. He was the only one who had a motorcycle and often rode it as a means of checking gas and oil lines in the Cook's forest area around Big Salmon Creek. Walking was necessary only in areas burdened with steep hills and creeks.

Nora was already married with two children when one night her father decided to check the oil line off Queens Road near Blair's Gap. As always, Nora helped her sisters and mother in Great-grandmother's kitchen, preparing the evening meal. It was a large family and there were many hungry men and children to be fed. Nora recalled the story as though it had happened yesterday. Two of Nora's brothers, Carl and Jim, affectionately known as Bake and Gooney, and her father—my great-grandfather—were several hours late for supper and the food was near the point of being spoiled. Nora could not recall a time before or after that her father was as upset as on that night in 1921 when he returned from Blair's Gap.

Clifton was visibly shaken and obviously uncomfortable talking about it. That was the only night Nora could remember that Great-grandfather's booming voice hadn't echoed with "Hello the house!" The children had not snapped to attention, as was customary upon Great-grandfather's arrival. The family slowly gathered around Clifton as he told of the events that had taken place earlier that evening. Supper was left to spoil. Only my great-grandfather's voice could be heard. His words shook as he spoke.

It was the time of year for lightning strikes and forest fires; the oil line that ran through Blair's Gap hadn't been checked for a couple of weeks. Although the line ran through terrain that prohibited motorcycle passage, Great-grandfather had heard reports of small fires in the area and knew it was important he check this section of line. Arrangements were made to meet a fellow employee, Charlie Black, just before dusk, when Great-grandfather anticipated reaching the end of the line. Charlie would wait with a company wagon to give him a ride back to the main office in Guitonville.

Bake and Gooney had stopped by United Natural Gas to walk home with their father after work. Upon learning that their father would be working late, Bake and Gooney accompanied Charlie to a pre-determined point in the trail where the gas line could be seen. The boys had been waiting in the wagon for what seemed a long time. A thunderstorm could be heard in the distance. It was getting near dark and the boys were getting worried about their father. Bake asked if they should start a fire so that their father could find his way back to the trail. Before anyone had a chance to respond, Gooney chimed in, "I'll collect some wood before it gets too dark to round it up." Just as Gooney jumped down off the wagon, Great-grandfather called to everyone from the woods, "Hello the wagon!"

Bake climbed over the buckboard seat to make room for his father and, from among a greasy selection of assorted wrenches, pipe cutters, and dies, began clearing a spot for Gooney and himself to sit. As my great-grandfather approached the clearing, Gooney walked over to greet him with a respectful handshake and smack on the shoulder. Upon reaching the wagon, Clifton apologized for being late and explained that several sections of line had been overgrown with brush and required clearing. Charlie acknowledged that he knew which sections of line Clifton was talking about and agreed to send a crew to clear the overgrowth within a couple of days. Great-grandfather and Gooney climbed in the wagon, and with a light snap and pull of the reins, Charlie proceeded to turn the wagon around and head back down the trail they had come in on only an hour earlier.

They had managed to get about two miles down the trail when they came to a wooden logging bridge that spanned a small creek running through Kelly Hill in an area known locally as Blair's Gap. Clifton noticed a small campfire about fifty yards down the side of the creek, grabbed the reins from Charlie, and stopped the wagon on the bridge.

It was not uncommon for travelers to camp in the woods as they were passing through and Clifton anticipated warning such a camper about the potential for forest fires since it was late in the summer and the brush was dry. Great-grandfather handed the reins back to Charlie and instructed the boys to wait in the wagon while he walked down to speak with what he anticipated to be an out-of-work traveler.

Great-grandfather climbed out of the wagon and made his way down the embankment that ran along the side of the bridge. The creek flowed in a small gully that denoted the area known as Blair's Gap. Parallel to Blair's Gap existed a small strip of land on either side of the creek that was fairly flat and overgrown with shrubs. Clifton maneuvered himself through the shrubs and toward the campfire. As he grew nearer, he saw the figure of a man sitting on what appeared to be the stump of a downed tree.

The man, dressed in the attire of an oil-field worker, looked as though he had fallen asleep while trying to warm himself. He wore a wide brim hat and a dark, three-quarter-length slicker that reached the top of his work boots. The man's arms were folded across his chest and his hands tucked under his elbows. His knees angled close to his torso with his feet tucked underneath close to the stump. His head appeared to be tilted forward so that Great-grandfather only saw the top of his hat. The man seemed to have a shotgun or walking stick resting horizontally across his lap. Black bears were common in the area, and Clifton had no intentions of startling a sleeping traveler that might well be armed.

Great-grandfather called to the traveler. "Hello the campfire! Hello, stranger!" No response. The campfire crackled between Great-grandfather and the traveler, and he was not sure the traveler would be able to see him where he stood. Clifton walked another ten or fifteen feet and again called to the traveler. "Hello the campfire! Hello stranger!" The traveler lifted his head slightly and said, "Come and warm yourself by the fire." The traveler did not seem at all out of place so Clifton maneuvered through the remaining ten or fifteen feet to the clearing where the traveler sat.

As Great-grandfather entered the clearing, he walked between two large wooden chests. It was only then that he realized the stranger was also sitting on a chest. The three chests were arranged in a circular fashion around the campfire. Great-grandfather surveyed the campsite, wondering if the man was truly alone. Although Clifton said nothing, he saw no horse and questioned how one man could have gotten three such chests so far out in the woods without help. Great-grandfather cautiously walked up to the fire and rubbed his hands together for warmth. The stranger unfolded his arms, leaned forward, retrieved a porcelain cup from in front of the fire, and emptied the contents of the cup onto the ground. Clifton watched with amazement as the stranger grabbed a pot of coffee from a rock next to the fire with his bare hands and proceeded to refill his cup. Surely this man must have worked in many oil fields for his hands to be so calloused that he could grab a steaming coffee pot.

The stranger again spoke to my great-grandfather, "Have a cup of coffee. I've been waiting to talk with you for a while, Clifton." The stranger's words made Great-grandfather uncomfortable and apprehensive. His stomach tightened as he took the cup from the stranger's hand. Who was this traveler and how did he know his name? Great-grandfather spoke firmly. "How is it that you know my name? I don't recognize your voice." The stranger taunted my great-grandfather as he poured another cup of coffee into a second cup that seemed to come from nowhere, "You've only known of me, Clifton. You haven't actually met me." The stranger lifted his head only slightly to take a sip of his coffee. Great-grandfather grew impatient and raised his voice. "Do not talk in riddles, stranger. If I should know of you, tell me who you are!"

Somewhere near this point of the recollection, Bake brought his obviously shaken father a glass of water and encouraged him to continue. Clifton took the glass in his big hand and slammed down half a glass of water as another man might slam down a glass of medicinal whiskey. He took in a deep breath, regained his composure, and continued.

The stranger again spoke to Great-grandfather. "I'm the one to whom you make no concession or sacrifice. Surely, you must have known that I would come." Great-grandfather could not respond. The stranger continued. "Come closer and you will surely recognize me. I'm he that you have feared and walked a wide arc around all these years."

Great-grandfather reluctantly stepped closer. The stranger tilted his head slightly, steadied his walking stick on the ground with his right hand, and stood. He was a small, bent-over, ill-shaped man. When the stranger made eye contact, Great-grandfather fell into a dark void that took over his every conscious thought. He searched the stranger's eyes for a sign of life and saw nothing. The man's eyes were black and absent of all emotion and feeling. My great-grandfather wanted to look away but could not. As events unfolded, Clifton could only watch what would take place. He felt as though he were an observer to the events taking place between the stranger and himself. Although he was aware of what was taking place, he had no ability to alter the events.

Great-grandfather and the stranger suddenly stood in front of one of the chests, which sat across from where the traveler first spoke to him and to the left of where Clifton first entered the camp. The traveler brought forth his walking stick and struck the base of the chest that was in front of them. The top of the chest flung open to reveal an abundance of gold coins, ingots, and chains. The traveler again spoke, saying, "This will soon be yours to spend as you will." Great-grandfather dropped his coffee and fell to his knees in disbelief. He thought of his family, how the gold would provide for them. He thought of quitting his job and never having to work again. As he reached to touch the gold, he found himself and the traveler in front of a second chest, the one to the right of where he entered the camp.

The traveler again brought forth his walking stick and struck the base of the second chest. The chest overflowed with red rubies. Great-grandfather, still on his knees, extended his right hand and caught a single ruby as it fell from the chest. The rubies were uniform in size and fit one to his hand.

As Great-grandfather examined the ruby, reflections of the campfire slowly gave way to the image of a beautiful woman. She lay on her back and slowly rolled from side to side. The longer he looked, the more detailed the image became. Her hands were clasped together over her head, and her body was draped in a transparent, scarf-like material. Great-grandfather watched as she seductively rubbed her knees together. He felt as though he were standing at her feet. He looked away to see the entire chest of rubies. Each contained the image of a different woman. As great-grandfather reached for a second ruby, he suddenly found himself and the traveler standing in front of the third chest.

The traveler again brought forth his walking stick and struck the base of the third chest. A brilliant sky-blue light sprang from the chest to the bottom of the treetops. The burst of light scared Great-grandfather, and he would have fallen completely backward from where he knelt if he had not caught himself with his hands. The contents of the third chest were brightly illuminated and difficult to discern. As Great-grandfather leaned forward to see the source of the blue light, his curiosity was stronger than his will to resist. The blue light was replaced with a thick white fog. At this point in the recollection, Nora recalled that tears welled up in her father's eyes. He informed the family that his thoughts were filled with greed and lust. He did not have the strength to turn away.

Without thought, Great-grandfather brought forth his right hand and brushed the thick fog aside. As his vision cleared, he knew he was seeing a premonition of things to come. He was in the main office of United Natural Gas. From his description, Nora said he was wearing what would later be known as a pinstripe zoot suit. Great-grandfather reclined in an oak office chair with his feet crossed atop the president's desk. His hands were folded in his lap, and his jacket hung open to expose a matching vest and gold watch chain.

He quickly snapped his feet to the floor when he heard a knock at the door. It was a familiar coworker dressed in coveralls and covered from head to toe in crude oil. Before my great-grandfather could explain what he was doing in the president's office, his coworker exclaimed, "We've just finished capping the well, boss. It looks like fifty barrels a day!" Great-grandfather looked around to see who his coworker was speaking to and saw nobody else in the room. When he realized his coworker had called him "boss," he found himself again staring into a thick white fog. He needed to know more. As Great-grandfather again brought forth his right hand to brush the fog aside, he found himself and the traveler standing next to the fire as they had been before the contents of the chests had been revealed.

The traveler again spoke, "All these things I have shown you and more will be yours if you but follow me a short distance into the woods." The traveler broke eye contact, turned, and walked into the woods. Unable to do anything else, Great-grandfather followed him. He knew the traveler by many names and where they were going, but he could do nothing to stop himself. He took another step and became aware of his surroundings. The woods were silent, and he was afraid. He heard a distant voice, calling, "Clifton! Where in God's name are you going?" There was a loud burst of thunder behind Great-grandfather. Clifton took his eyes off the traveler and looked over his left shoulder. Lightning flashed, and he saw the outline of Charlie and the boys on the logging bridge.

Charlie was yelling, "This way Clifton!" Great-grandfather turned further around and looked back to the campfire. The blazing fire he had anticipated seeing was just a barely noticeable pile of red embers and there was no sign of the expected smoke. It was as though someone had kicked the fire out several hours ago. He realized the chests were now stumps. He spun back around to look for the traveler, but there was only darkness. The voices were now clear. "Over here. This way, Dad. This way, Clifton!" Great-grandfather turned toward the familiar voices of his coworker and sons. Then he began to run. His feet quickly cut a path through the bushes and the briers.

The next thing Great-grandfather remembered was riding in the wagon. Bake reached from behind him and squeezed his shoulder. "We weren't sure if you could find your way back. It got pretty dark after you kicked out the fire." The ride back was quiet, and Great-grandfather didn't remember much of the conversation. He returned home and shared his recollection.

The events of that night had been a horrifying experience for Nora's father. In addition to working fulltime for United Natural Gas, Clifton was a preacher at the Guitonville Church of God. His wife and children literally attended church twice on Sundays. It was not a family known to tell lies. Clifton was appalled he had been so easily lured into following the traveler into the woods. The comfort and security that his faith had brought him were now in jeopardy. He had seen the devil, and it had caused him to question the strength of his unshakable faith. Although my great-grandfather's words would remain with her for the rest of her life, Nora never again asked her father about the events of that night. Since Great-grandfather was a preacher, I cannot help but wonder what a prize he would have been to the devil if he had followed the traveler into the woods that night.

Unknown to anyone at the time, my great-grandfather's encounter in the woods that night was not the end of anything; rather, it was the beginning and foretelling of a generational curse.

3

MOTHER'S TABLE

The Catalyst

From as early as I could remember, my mother was a nurse, first surgical and then an emergency room nurse. Always, she had a big heart and empathy for the suffering of others. As I grew to know my mother as a person, I discovered that she was also an open-minded woman of Polish heritage who successfully strived to raise her children with open minds and an unshakable Christian faith. Mom began talking to Alfreido when I was only ten or eleven years old. The family was introduced to Alfreido through my mother's table, and the table became an old and familiar friend. Although I remember vividly my mother's first encounter with Alfreido, I can't recall when she first began to use the table.

The table was a sort of advanced Ouija board that progressed from a round end table with lettered tabs of paper to a larger three-foot diameter table with permanently mounted, letter-engraved pieces of plastic. The table accommodated each letter of the alphabet and pieces for "Yes" and "No." Numbers were counted by revolutions around the table. Alfreido had a special wine glass that was always pre-warmed by candle before use. After warming, the glass was placed upside-down in the center of the table, and at least three people—my mother being one—placed the tip of their pinkie finger on the inverted base of the wine glass. After a few minutes of concentration, the glass would inevitably begin to move, sluggish at first, then faster. My mother would begin, "Is that you, Alfreido?" The glass would move to the word "Yes." My mother would then continue with her questions.

The table was called upon two or three times a month, and questions were generally pre-planned or follow-up to information previously provided by Alfreido. During a table session, my mother was always the orchestrator of the proceedings and often asked questions about life after death, heaven, angels, and the spiritual realm. Much of my early understanding of the spiritual realm came from those table sessions. On occasion, our questions were about Alfreido. We asked when he was born, under what circumstances he died, where he had lived, and how he had come to live in limbo. Despite having no personal computers or Internet to verify what Alfreido was saying, historical information was often verified with minimal effort at the local library. Questions concerning personal gain or profit were never asked or discussed.

Alfreido continued to talk with my mother, and it made no difference whether I joined her at the table or not. In addition to predicting such things as Nixon defeating Johnson in 1968 or when our family would receive the next letter from my cousin in Vietnam, Alfreido spoke of his own experiences battling the Cuban guerrillas in the Ten Years' War between Spain and Cuba. Alfreido consistently provided my mother with information that could be researched and validated or confirmed as accurate with minimal effort. Gradually, I became a believer. The more he spoke, the less I doubted him.

By the time I reached the age of eleven, my mother was quite comfortable entertaining friends and family with the table. Friends of my parents were well aware of my mother's use of the table and knew that with just a little coaxing, she could be talked into what they loosely referred to as a séance. For whatever reason and regardless of the spirit that my mother believed she had contacted, whenever my father walked into the room, the glass would go nuts.

My father was a decorated Korean War veteran, a prison guard at Attica, and a strict disciplinarian at home. Perhaps the spirits didn't care for him because he was a black-and-white man with little time for what he considered imaginary and not worth his effort. The glass had been known to go over the edge of the table, circle the underside of the table, return to the top of the table, and circle the table at speeds that would oftentimes leave our pinkies behind. One or two such experiences were enough to convince my father that he would rather watch than participate. In hindsight, I realize there was a reason for the bizarre behavior of the glass.

Occasionally, when my parents weren't entertaining guests, my sister and I would join my mother at the table. For as long as I can remember, the table always required at least three people to operate. To my surprise, my mother one day asked me to join her at the table, just the two of us. That was the night we first met Alfreido. Not much happened at first, and then the glass began to slowly move. At that time, I wasn't sure if my mother was pushing the glass or I was. Then she asked the spirit for its name. I remember deliberately pushing the glass to the letter "A," then "L," then "F," until I spelled out the name Alfreido. The name came to me as I spelled it. I had not planned it in advance and had no idea what urge had forced me to spell that particular name, let alone any name.

The spirit was apparently happy with the name I had selected for him, and Alfreido gradually became the only spirit my mother relied upon. I didn't have a clear idea at the time of how psychic abilities manifested themselves. Nor did I fully recognize the significance of the fact that the glass would traverse the table without a third party. I do, however, admit to feeling somewhat uneasy about operating the table with just the two of us. I knew that what we were doing was peculiar and different. As I recall, my mother and I were the only two people able to operate the table without a third party. I never had the heart to tell her I had physically pushed the glass to spell out the name "Alfreido."

After my mother's success at operating the table with two people, she began to encourage what she called my "abilities." If Mom expected a relative to come over for a visit or she was waiting for a package in the mail, she would ask me to go upstairs and consult the Ouija board. I remember my first attempt at this. Mom wanted to know when our television would be back from the repairman. It was only after I had the Ouija board out and set up in my lap at the top of the stairs that Thursday stuck in my mind. I spelled out "Thursday" with the viewer just as I had spelled out "Alfreido" with the wine glass. I put the board away, went downstairs, and told my mother that our television would be back on the following Thursday.

Sure enough, the repairman returned with our television on the following Thursday. That got me wondering. *Who exactly is running the Ouija board?* Was I pushing the viewer because I subconsciously knew the answers, or was someone else telling me the answers that I transferred to the viewer? It scared me to realize I had asked myself a question with no clear black-or-white answer. I was slowly losing the world I understood, the one I could explain.

At first, my mother viewed my solitary Ouija performances as a sort of novelty. As time went on and the string of successes increased, she and I became increasingly uneasy with the spirit behind the board. Although my mother and I never discussed our uneasiness, I believe the discomfort was most deeply rooted in me. By now, I knew a spirit wasn't speaking to me through the Ouija board, but rather, it was a spirit speaking to me directly. I had no concept of the ramifications and the doorways that might be inadvertently opened by my ignorance.

I was an altar boy during this period of my life, and I was happy to serve whenever called upon. I viewed the 4:30 a.m. mass each morning as a personal sacrifice I was happy to make because I felt as though I was doing something to please God. As I recall, we typically had more people working at the altar than we had sitting in the pews. The Sunday morning mass was a different story. Sundays seemed more like a ritual for the congregation than a sacrifice to God.

Right or wrong, I was a rebellious Catholic. When I could not substantiate the things I was taught about being a Catholic in the Bible, I questioned them. That might sound pompous, but I loved God and just wanted to please Him. I was puzzled by a Catholic doctrine that taught if you weren't in heaven, hell, or purgatory, you weren't dead. If that were true, who were these spirits my mother and I spoke with? Now that I've read the Bible a few times, I wonder how purgatory even became part of the discussion.

My mother was a graduate of a Catholic nursing school, a member of the Holy Rosary Society, attended church on Sundays, and encouraged my participation as an altar boy. How could she hold so tightly to her Roman Catholic beliefs and at the same time so openly accept the existence of Alfreido? For that matter, how could I? I never questioned my mother's beliefs. My mother wasn't capable of misinterpretation, and a little boy couldn't possibly be expected to understand the teachings of the church. I was truly at odds with myself and pulled between two worlds.

My father was close-minded and set in his ways. Most spirits, Alfreido included, didn't much like my father. They would always say, "He didn't believe in them or the table" and for the most part, they were right. Dad was raised in a religious family, but he wasn't a Catholic and hadn't maintained any religious affiliation since leaving the army. He didn't really have a firm footing in either world. My father often suggested that mom had been pushing the glass. Such a suggestion would cause Alfreido to go spastic. Secretly, I also questioned the validity of the glass. If I dreamed up the name "Alfreido" and I knowingly manipulated the Ouija board, what would make me think that any of this was real?

If the contact were real, how would I come to terms with it? My Catholic background and introduction to Bible study made me leery. I recalled the verse, "*Be sober, be vigilant; because your adversary the devil, as a roaring lion, walks about, looking for whom he may devour*" (1 Peter 5:8). Within a year, I had put aside my solitaire Ouija performances and attempted to join the ranks of my father as an observer rather than a participant. Although I might occasionally be coaxed into participating when a third party was needed at the table, for the most part, my gut told me to abstain. I retired completely from the Ouija board and two-party table sessions.

Alfreido lulled us into a passive acceptance of talking with familiar spirits and opened the door to let the traveler into the room when our guards were down. Aware of the recollection since childhood, my father and his cousin, Dick, knew of the traveler long before any of the rest of us. Dick's wife, my mother, and I had all spoken with him in Ohio long before we heard anything of the recollection. Once I had returned home, my father's mother told me about the recollection and described the traveler in the woods. I assumed Dick had told his wife about the recollection just as my father had told my mother about the recollection. Once I knew about it, I knew that the traveler in Ohio was one and the same as the traveler in the woods.

My mother continued to talk with Alfreido exclusively until the summer of 1971. It was in that summer my father and his longtime friend and cousin Dick were invited to meet the traveler at Blair's Gap. Although my mother never showed any sign of being shaken or made any declaration that she was through with the table, she never again used the table after that night in 1971. My mother recognized the spirit behind the table, and it wasn't Alfreido.

It's easy now to look back and think about how things might have turned out differently. Perhaps I wouldn't have stepped so far out of the light if I had known then what I know now. Perhaps I needed to see the dark to appreciate the light. Many things in my life have driven me to read the Bible from cover to cover, over and over. Now I see how something done so innocently by the unaware can so easily open a door to something not so innocent.

The Bible is clear on the consequences of speaking with familiar spirits. "*And when they shall say to you, seek unto them that have familiar spirits, and unto wizards that peep and that mutter; should not a people seek unto their God, for the living to the dead? To the law and to the testimony: if they speak not according to the word, it is because there is no light in them. And they shall pass through it hardly bestead and hungry: they shall fret themselves, and curse their king and their God, and look upward. And they shall look unto the earth; and behold trouble and darkness, dimness and anguish; and they shall be driven to darkness*" (*Isaiah 8:19–22*).

An avid reader of Edgar Cayce, visitor to Lily Dale, and fan all things spiritual, my mother had no idea of the fire we played with. At eleven years old, I couldn't even begin to imagine the doors that we were opening or the forces that we were unleashing through my mother's table.

4

THE APPOINTMENT

Into the Darkness

If I had to set a point in time when this recurring nightmare known as Blair's Gap had started, it would have been when the appointment was made—the same night I saw the traveler and received God's reassurance of the presence of evil. As a child, I could not grasp the significance of what had happened or put into words how the loss of my innocence impacted me. Things were not as they seemed, and the world was no longer the safe place I had grown up in. I had been made aware of choices that seemed beyond my ability to fully comprehend.

As an adult, I can now put the events of that night into proper perspective. At the time, I wondered if I should take a bite of that large and juicy, Red Delicious, satisfying and refreshing apple that was so plain to see and so ready to fall from the tree, or should I walk away? Could I just walk away? Could my wonderment and curiosity ever be satisfied now that I knew what was possible and what was real? I stood at that crossroads for many years in my life.

My father and his cousin Dick remained close friends despite seldom being able to spend much time together as adults. They had known each other since childhood and together they shared many exploits and adventures. Dick was one of few men capable of drinking one-for-one with my father. When they got together, they drank a lot of beer and told a lot of stories. Sometimes they drank as fuel for new adventures like becoming the only two veterans to ever be kicked out of the Marienville VFW for being drunk and disorderly.

I was with Dick once when he jokingly tried to pass my dad on a single-lane highway. He raced down the dirt shoulder of the road and grinned from ear to ear. We were going forty-five to fifty miles an hour when Dick decided to make his move. He pulled alongside my father, smiled, gave the car some gas, and took off. My father wasn't a man to back off. When Dick gave it some gas, he gave it some gas. Soon we were barreling down the shoulder at seventy miles an hour, fishtailing, and stirring up a cloud of dirt and debris. I suppose I should have been a little scared, but I wasn't. I knew that they were harmless; half of everything Dick and my father did they did for show. They had their limits and my safety was never in question. Dick drove at that speed for a few seconds, made no attempt to actually pass my father, slammed on the brakes, slid sideways down the shoulder of the road, and pulled back in behind my father. Dick and my dad drove the rest of the way home at close to the speed limit. Seldom ever getting into any real trouble, they did things like that for fun.

Dick and my father were such close friends that my mother and Dick's wife, Donna, couldn't help but be friends as well. Our families shared a lot of good times together. Dick's family had spent their summer vacation with our family in 1970, and it was our turn to spend our summer vacation with his family in 1971. My sister was a year older than me and considerably more trusted by my parents. She was asked to stay home to take care of our pets and keep our grandmother company.

Shared vacations were typically a week long, and we had a lot of things to do and see in a short period of time. Dick and Donna had planned a visit to an Indian gravesite for the first day of our vacation. That was usually the way vacations went. We'd all have an adventure during the day, and then the adults would drink and shoot the breeze at night. At least that was the way it was for my mother and Donna. Most times, my father and Dick drank during the adventure. The gravesite was located in a park-like setting, driving distance from Dick and Donna's place in Newark, Ohio. Donna and my mother packed a picnic lunch. Dick and my father packed a cooler. The park contained a meadow of large mounds, thought to be massive Indian grave structures.

On the second day, we saw Big Muskie, the largest earth-moving device in operation at the time. The bucket could hold something like 660 standing men. I was quite impressed. By Thursday, we had also visited the World War II Air Force museum, two returned space capsules, and the Ohio State Fair. The adults were ready to stay home and take it easy by Friday. I spent the day playing catch with my dad and Dick who alternated between drinking and tossing the ball. We all enjoyed a nice picnic lunch and generally just had a good time in each other's company.

By nightfall, Dick and Donna's children were in bed and my father was sitting in the backyard, swapping stories. Each of my father's stories would inevitably be followed by one of Dick's stories. Dick was retired from the Air Force and had worked for NASA at one time. He had my father and I convinced that the US government was capable of actually shrinking objects, just like in the movie *Fantastic Voyage*. The only problem, according to Dick, was that they couldn't bring them back. Dick used terms like "infinitely small point of original mass." My father and

I weren't necessarily that impressed by the fact that Dick worked for NASA, but words like "infinite" and "mass" were enough to convince us that Dick knew what he was talking about.

The mood was right. Everybody was talking and having a good time. After a while, Dick and Donna began asking my mother about the table. Within an hour, my mother had agreed to have a table session. Donna searched for a wine glass while my mother and I prepared paper letters for the makeshift table. Donna cleared a round table of plants, placed a candle in the center of the table, and held a wine glass in her hand before my mother and I were ready to Scotch Tape the letters. Dick had located three folding chairs to sit around the table. There was never any question about who was going to sit at the table. Dick and my father stood back against the counter that separated the living room from the kitchen drinking beer.

Donna, my mother, and I prepared the table. After the letters were taped to the table, my mother warmed the wine glass over the candle in a sort of upside-down swirling motion, something like a professional wine taster might do. Dick offered to let my mother use his Zippo lighter. Dick and my father then laughed like hell. Donna said something to Dick and he agreed he wouldn't say anything that might further upset the "spirits."

My mother placed the wine glass in the center of the table and passed the candle to Donna, who sat it on top of the television. My mother instructed Donna and I to place the tip of our right pinkie on the inverted base of the wine glass. She began by saying, "Is there anybody here?"

Within a minute, the glass began to move. I noticed very quickly that the glass seemed distant, not like Alfreido. A few questions later, my mother noticed. Mom asked, "Is that you, Alfreido? You don't seem yourself tonight." The glass slowly traced the circumference of the table and came to a stop at "NO."

"What is your name?" my mother asked. The glass paused as if to think for a second and then moved to the letter "M." Our pinkies followed the glass to "Y," then "N," then "A," until the spirit had answered, "M-Y-N-A-M-E-I-S-N-O-T-I-M-P-O-R-T-A-N-T." Dick burst out in contagious laughter, followed by my father. "Come on," Dick asked in a light-hearted manner, "You're pushing that glass, aren't you, Anita?" My mother wasn't offended, but Donna gently scolded Dick, and Dick and my father again agreed to behave and try not to offend the spirits.

My mother continued. "What is wrong tonight? Don't you want to talk to us?" The spirit responded, "D-I-C-K-D-O-N-T-B-E-L-I-E-V-E." Dick replied, "If you are real, show us a sign!" Neither my mother nor I had ever issued such a challenge. Mom looked at me, raised her eyebrows, smiled, and put her pinkie on the glass. Donna and I followed suit.

Mom continued, "Will you show us a sign?" The spirit answered, "C-O-N-C-E-N-T-R-A-T-E." Mom left the glass in the middle of the table, and Dick and my father agreed to be serious and attempt to concentrate. We concentrated for fifteen minutes. I know it was fifteen minutes because Dick made mention of it. Then we heard the sirens.

We heard the distant sounds of a rescue squad and fire truck and temporarily forgot about the table. Dick was the first to notice the sirens drawing closer. "Sounds like they're headed in our direction." Dick and Donna lived in a mobile home in the outside center lot of a large U-shaped trailer park. As you faced the road in front of their home, the rescue squad and fire truck came to a stop at the right-hand entrance to the park. That got our attention.

Donna and my mother leaned out the front door and I looked out the living room window. Dick and my father stood on the front steps. One of them suggested we should walk down and check it out. After walking around the bend in the road, we saw the flashing lights of the rescue squad and fire truck. It was a large trailer park with large lots and it had taken us a few minutes to walk to the accident. The sirens were silent. A car had flipped over on its roof in a gully across from the park entrance.

Probably twenty sightseers had gathered by the time we got there. The driver had already been extracted from the car and taken to the rescue squad. The car was in a semi-wooded area, and the radio was still playing. I heard some kid yell, "Get the battery. It's worth five bucks!" No one took notice of his remark. We stood around for a minute talking about how fast the driver must have been going and what must have occurred to cause the car to wind up in the ditch. At some point on the way back to the trailer, the conversation changed back to the table and whether we should be more specific about our request for a sign.

Dick suggested we ask the spirit to ring the phone. Everyone agreed that was a good idea. My mother offered the challenge and the spirit responded, "C-O-N-C-E-N-T-R-A-T-E." Everyone concentrated on the phone. Within five minutes, the phone rang. The first ring startled everyone. By the third ring, the room was full of nervous laughter and Dick told me to pick it up and answer it. The sound I heard was similar to the loud hissing sound you hear when the TV cable goes out. There was no one on the line, and after a few seconds, I put the receiver back on the hook.

We decided to be even more specific. We asked the spirit to ring the phone three times. Within two minutes, the phone rang three times and then stopped. We asked again and again. We asked the spirit to ring the phone three times; then four times; then two times. Each time the phone rang as we requested. Responses came more rapidly and required less and less concentration. This went on for close to forty-five minutes.

Then we heard the sirens again. This time, the rescue squad and fire truck came to a stop at the left-hand entrance. Again, after walking around the bottom of the U-shaped access road, we saw the flashing lights. The sirens were again silent. Again, a car had flipped over on its roof in a gully across from the entrance. There were probably twenty sightseers standing around. The driver had already been extracted from the car and loaded into the rescue squad. Once again, the car was in a semi-wooded area, and the radio was playing. I heard some kid yell, "Get the battery. It's worth five bucks!"

No one seemed to take notice of the kid or the similarities between the two accidents. Perhaps they did and just weren't saying anything. It was like we had traveled into an alternate universe where all the rules had changed and time had slowed down. I wondered if I was the only one who heard the kid yell, "Get the battery. It's worth five bucks!"

Did I imagine the similarities? I wondered if the second accident could possibly be confirmation that the first was an answer to a requested, but unspecified sign. I kept these thoughts to myself as we walked back to the trailer. Dick was intrigued by the possibility that the spirit might actually be real. The conversation quickly turned to discussing the possibility that the spirit might actually be ringing the phone.

As soon as we sat back down at the table, Dick urged my mother to ask the spirit to let us see him. My mother placed her pinkie on the base of the wine glass. Donna and I followed suit. Mother asked, "Will you manifest yourself for us?" Letter by letter, the spirit responded, "I-W-I-L-L-M-A-K-E-M-Y-S-E-L-F-S-E-E-N-T-O-V-A-N-C-E-A-N-D-D-I-C-K." My mother then asked, "When will you make yourself seen to Vance and Dick?" The spirit replied, "S-E-P-T-E-M-B-E-R." The glass then circled the table thirteen times and came to a stop in the center.

My mother asked, "September 13?" The glass moved to "YES." My mother continued. "Where will you make yourself seen to Vance and Dick?" The spirit replied, "B-L-A-I-R-S-G-A-P."

Dick and my father were very familiar with Nora's recollection and now they knew with whom they were speaking. My mother asked, "Are you an evil spirit?" The spirit responded, "I-A-M-O-N-E-O-F-M-A-N-Y-M-Y-M-A-S-T-E-R-S-N-U-M-B-E-R-S-A-R-E-A-L-E-G-I-O-N." My mother took her hand away from the glass and placed it in her lap. Donna heard my father and Dick discussing Blair's Gap and encouraged them to continue. Donna had never heard the recollection and was curious about Blair's Gap. Her questions evoked my father's third-hand recollection. After recalling Nora's recollection, my father and Dick began to discuss the possibility of actually going to Blair's Gap. Not knowing if it was a conscious decision or unconscious decision, the glass was quietly put away.

Donna and my mother stayed inside while Dick and my father went outside to further discuss the details of possibly going to Blair's Gap. Donna said something about Dick and my father being like a couple of kids when they got together. My mother agreed and commented on enjoying being able to see Vance so happy.

About twenty minutes had gone by when Dick came in and said something about my father. He spoke as he came through the door. "Hey, Anita, Vance is acting kind of strange." My mother was sitting on the sofa and turned to hear what he was saying. Dick said, "He's just . . . talking to himself."

My mother came to her feet as my father walked through the front door. He was as white as a sheet and very serious. Mom asked, "Are you okay, Vance?" He paused for a second and replied, "I was talking to my dad." Mom asked, "What did your father say, Vance?" It was then that my father realized what he was saying and that everyone was listening and watching him. He abruptly answered, "I don't want to talk about it." After a few questions, it became clear my father really didn't want to talk about it. Donna and my mother let it go.

Dick suggested that he and my father compare work schedules and available vacations to see if a meeting at Blair's Gap would be possible in September. As it turned out, September 13 fell on a Monday. Dick and my father agreed they would meet on Saturday, September 11.

They both had the eleventh and twelfth off and planned to take the following Monday and Tuesday as vacation. My mother reminded my father that I had to start school on September 8. My father responded as I had hoped he would. "With his grades, I am sure it won't make any difference one way or another if he misses a couple of days." I knew his remark wasn't a compliment, but I liked his answer anyway. I wanted to go camping with the guys. I enjoyed their company, and I had a lot of fun around Dick and my dad when they were drinking. I may have been a little apprehensive, but I certainly wasn't scared of going as I was sure no spirits would manifest themselves in the woods for two drunken cousins—not without my mother's influence. What I knew for sure was that this trip would be a good time and an adventure to remember.

It was getting late and my shirt smelled like sweat from playing catch that afternoon. I decided to take a shower and get ready for bed. Although I tried not to show my fear, I was quite shaken by what had happened. I convinced myself that Dick and my father had somehow arranged with a neighbor to have the phone ring. I wondered if all that concentration had caused Donna and my mother's imagination to spill over to the glass. The more I tried to provide myself with explanations, the more I became aware of my excuses, and the harder it became to dispute what we had seen.

I wanted to know the truth about what we believed we saw and heard that evening, but at the same time, I was a little afraid of what I might find out. I secretly decided to test the spirit. I would try to confirm or dispute the presence of evil. I wanted to know. It had recently been Donna's birthday, and she still had four or five birthday cards standing on the counter above and behind the television.

As I walked past the counter on the way to the bathroom, I chose one of the cards. I selected the card in my mind, never touched it, and said nothing to anyone. I spoke to myself. "If there really is an evil spirit here, let this card fall over onto the television while I am taking a shower." Just as quickly, I knew I would not be convinced. I saw myself making excuses and blaming a gust of wind for the fallen card.

I selected a second card. Again, I spoke to myself and never touched the card. "If there is really an evil spirit here, let both of these cards fall onto the television while I am taking a shower." I had selected two cards that were not side-by-side. If the wind blew them over, it would have to leave a card standing between them.

It had been a scorching hot day and the front door had been left open all evening to catch a small breeze. As if to make it even more difficult and harder to dispute, as I walked past the open door, I again spoke to myself. "If there is truly an evil spirit here, let the door be closed and the two cards I selected fall over onto the television while I am taking a shower."

When I closed the bathroom door, I realized I was alone for the first time that evening. Unfortunately, I didn't feel alone. I felt a presence with me. I was very uncomfortable with the idea of being so far from everyone in the living room. I felt vulnerable and unprotected. Even so, I got undressed and prepared to take my shower. I planned on making it a quick one. I was in a hurry to get back to the living room, where I might again feel safe and secure with all the other people.

I got undressed, climbed into the tub, closed the curtains, adjusted the water, and turned on the shower. I closed my eyes and began to soap my face. Suddenly, my uneasiness and vulnerability became almost unbearable. I felt as though someone were watching me. I quickly rinsed my face and finished my shower. At some point while drying myself, I decided to stop and comb my hair before leaving the bathroom. The mirror was covered with fog and condensation. I wiped a circle in the center of the mirror with my dry towel. As I wiped the mirror, I saw a man sitting behind me on the washing machine, just over my left shoulder. He was looking at the floor. His clothes were dark. He wore a long trench coat and wide brim hat. He began to lift his head. Before we made eye contact, I turned around in fright. There was no one there.

I got dressed with my back to the mirror so I could keep my eyes on the washer and dryer. I threw my towel on the dryer and headed up the hall to see if I had the courage to tell anyone about the man I had just seen in the bathroom. As I reached the end of the hall, I looked up at Donna who was standing in the kitchen. Just then, the front door slammed shut. Dick said something about the wind really picking up. I looked at the counter to see if the gust from the door had blown the cards over. Only the two cards I had selected were missing. As I entered the living room, I saw the cards. They were lying face down, just in front of the counter, on the television. I was too scared to say anything.

After sitting on the couch and saying nothing for nearly ten minutes, I realized my behavior was out of the ordinary. It was out of character for me to sit still and keep my mouth shut. My father had raised me to suck it up and take it like a man. I was trying my best to keep my composure, but I was scared, and if anyone was looking, they could have read it on my face. I just couldn't get it together so I did what I thought was the next best thing, I excused myself to go to bed. That was a stupid idea. I found myself alone with my thoughts and my mind was racing. There was no possibility of my falling asleep.

Looking back now, I find it odd that nobody was talking about the table or what had happened that evening, as was to be expected following one of my mother's table sessions. It was as though we were all in a haze or a dream. Remembering what I saw in the bathroom that night and my father talking with his father, I wonder now if we all may have seen our own private glimpse of hell that night. Unfortunately, I am the only remaining survivor, and there is nobody left to ask.

After I went to bed, things quieted down. There was a stereo in the room, and when Dick walked down the hall, I asked him if I could listen to the radio. He stepped into the room and turned on the radio. Dick told me that I could listen to it as long as I shut it off before I fell asleep. I promised I would. It was comforting to hear another voice and something to distract me from my thoughts. I listened intently to every word and every song. I must have listened to that radio for two hours before I fell asleep. The next thing I remember was Dick waking me up when he came in the room to shut off the stereo. "I thought I told you to shut this off before you fell asleep." I apologized for forgetting and fell back asleep easily the second time.

When I got up on Saturday morning, the trailer was empty. I heard muffled conversations from out back and walked down the hall to look out Dick and Donna's bedroom window. The adults were all sitting in lawn chairs, sipping coffee. The children were on top of the picnic table, playing with a large, inflatable

Seagram's liquor bottle. I combed my hair and hurried out back to catch up on the conversations.

Dick and my father were talking about how they would coordinate their trip to Blair's Gap, and Donna and my mother were comparing work schedules. Nobody made mention of the invitation or what had brought about Dick and my father's desire to go to Blair's Gap. From all outside appearances, it was just a normal day, like nothing at all out of the ordinary had happened.

Everyone's behavior seemed odd to me as a child. As an adult, I've been told that alcoholics often use avoidance as a means of coping with all things uncomfortable. Whatever the reason, the adults playing down the events of the night before had eased my trepidation and fear.

Sometime around when my father stated he would borrow his father-in-law's truck camper for the trip, Donna and my mother had made it clear they weren't going. I doubt that Donna or my mother were afraid of going; quite the contrary, I think the idea of camping in the woods for three or four days and nights just didn't seem like fun. Besides, the spirit said he would show himself to Dick and my father, not to Donna or my mother.

Although I was never asked, I was always included in the plans and knew I was meant to go. I was excited about being included with the big boys on one of their adventures. The camper had two makeshift queen-size beds and would be plenty big enough for Dick, my father, and myself, even if I had to sleep on the floor. Donna would stay home with her children, and my mother would save her vacation and work.

Later that afternoon, I asked Donna if I could borrow her bicycle to go for a ride. My mother and father were talking about packing for the ride back to New York on the following morning, and I wanted to enjoy my time left in Ohio. Although things would change as I got older, at the time, it didn't bother me at all that Donna owned a full-size ladies' bike, complete with a bell and basket. Besides, nobody knew me in Ohio. The basket would serve nicely for collecting some local rock samples. I fancied myself as sort of an amateur geologist and had several dresser drawers full of rocks at home to prove it.

By the time I made it to the banks of the Licking River, I had only found one or two rocks worthy of keeping. I came to a stop and straddled the bicycle on the shoulder of the road. The banks of the river looked like a bonanza. It was a forty-foot incline down to the river, and the entire bank was a smorgasbord of rocks. Rocks were gray and ranged in size from that of a baseball to a little smaller than a soccer ball. I placed the kickstand down and climbed over the guardrail to check it out.

After examining two or three samples I found close to the shoulder of the road, I caught a glimmer of light out of the corner of my eye. Something further down the river and along the shoreline reflected the sun in my direction. The light was bright enough that I couldn't discern the source of the reflection. At first I thought it was a broken piece of glass or a bottle that had washed up along the shoreline.

I carefully made my way down to the shoreline. As I got closer to the source of light, I realized it was not a single reflection, but rather a group of smaller reflections. To my amazement, as I drew closer, I realized it was a rock. It was a rock like no other rock I had ever seen before. The rock was flat, about an inch and a half thick, and half the size of a monopoly board. It was dark gray and covered on the top with rounded concave indents that fit perfectly to the tips of my fingers. The bottom of each indent was a dark-green, glass-like material that had been the source of the reflections I had seen.

The rock was large and heavy and I knew I would never be able to carry it back to the trailer. It was all I could do to pick it up. Even if I managed to carry it up to the road, the rock would be too cumbersome to transport in the bicycle basket and would no doubt damage Donna's bike. I attempted to slam it down to break it over the edge of another rock. This proved more difficult than I had imagined. The rock was hard, and it took several attempts before it broke. I tried to break off a piece the size of a book. What I wound up with was a piece the size of my fist. The piece contained thirteen dark-green, glass-like divots. I climbed back up the hill and placed the fist-sized rock in the bicycle basket with my earlier finds.

I was in a hurry to get back to the trailer and show everyone my treasures. I rode the bicycle up the driveway, alongside Dick and Donna's trailer, where I found my parents still in the backyard, sitting side by side in lawn chairs. Dick and Donna were sitting about ten feet away on the picnic table bench, facing my parents. I placed the kickstand down, grabbed the indented rock, and walked over to show it to my father.

As I described the rock and what I had gone through to get it, my father reached out, and I handed it to him. My father rolled the rock around in the palm of his right hand, placed the rock in his left hand, and fit the tip of his right index finger into several of the indents. He then placed the rock back in his right hand and tilted it so that the dark-green indents became brighter as they caught the light of the sun. He spoke to my mother as he handed the rock to her. "What do you think now?" My mother smiled, tilted her head, and lifted her eyebrows as if to shrug her shoulders.

By that time, Dick and Donna were on their feet and walking over to see the rock for themselves. My mother handed the rock to Dick. Dick handled the rock in much the same manner as my father. I was surprised by the amount of interest the rock had generated among the adults.

I asked my father what he had meant by his comment to my mother. He told me to ask her. I turned to my mom, and she paused for a second before she answered. "We were talking about your dad's father talking to him last night. He warned your father not to go to Blair's Gap, but said if he and Dick went anyway, he would send thirteen green eyes to watch over and protect him. We didn't know what he was talking about. I thought he was joking." From that point forward, the rock became my father's.

We loaded up the car and headed back to New York the following morning. The ride was uneventful. I spent the remainder of the summer riding my go-cart, roller-skating, camping in the backyard, and doing chores around the house, always in quiet anticipation of our planned September trip to Blair's Gap.

What none of us knew then, and what would take me nearly another fifty years to recognize, was that the events of that night in Ohio would profoundly impact the lives of everyone who participated in the séance. My mother never again conducted a table session and died a painful death of lung cancer at an early age; my father remarried a convicted murderer and spiraled downhill for another ten years before dying of liver disease. Dick and Donna had their own problems, and here is my story.

5

ATTICA

The Devil's Handshake

On the weekend before our planned trip to Blair's Gap, my father drove to Elba, New York, and borrowed my grandfather's truck camper. He had swapped shifts with another prison guard and would be working days during the week prior to our trip. We had the camper stationed beside the house, all packed and ready to go by Tuesday morning. The plan was for us to leave sometime Saturday, September 11, meet Dick in Marienville, Pennsylvania, set up camp in or around Blair's Gap on Sunday, September 12, and spend Monday and Tuesday, September 13 and 14 at Blair's Gap to see who would come to see us and what would happen.

I started tenth grade on a Wednesday, the week before our planned excursion. By my second class on Thursday, I began hearing rumors of trouble at Attica. Many of my classmate's fathers were also guards at Attica and stories spread quickly. There had been a riot that morning. Several sections of the prison had been taken over by the inmates, and many guards had been taken hostage.

I went straight home after school that day. It was close to four in the afternoon when I walked up the driveway and noticed the camper wasn't sitting on the jacks next to the house where it used to be. Grandfather's camper was hooked to the back of my father's truck and apparently ready to go. When my father worked days, he usually arrived home at about 4:00 p.m. I expected him home soon.

I found my mother in the kitchen making sandwiches. She had been waiting for my sister and me to return from school. Patricia was just a few minutes behind me. When she got home, Mom told us that Dad was okay, but there had been some trouble at the prison and he would have to work late. He had called and asked her to bring him a couple of packs of cigarettes and something to eat. Mom asked us to ride along.

The prison parking lot was full to capacity. My mother drove around for several minutes, looking for a place to park. Just as she suggested we attempt to find an empty parking space at the bar across the street, Patricia spotted a car pulling out of a stall near the front gate. Mom quickly drove over and positioned her car so that she could see Dad when he came out. Guards were going in and coming out every few seconds.

We probably waited for another forty-five minutes before I saw my father. Mom got out of the car and waved him over. "Vance . . . over here!" He walked over, slid into the front passenger seat, gave my mother a kiss, and asked her what she had brought him to eat. My mother handed him a couple of large, wrapped sandwiches and a thermos of coffee. While he ate, he told us what had happened in the prison.

When the riot first started, there were less than 100 guards on duty to supervise 2,250 prisoners. It began at about 8:30 a.m. when a group of inmates refused to line up for a work detail. Armed only with their clubs, the attending guards were greatly outnumbered and easily overpowered. Moving swiftly, the convicts rushed through three out of four of the cellblocks and set fire to six buildings. The chapel, prison school, and machine shop were completely gutted. Quickly producing knives, pipes, baseball bats, and makeshift spears, the inmates captured guards and civilian employees as hostages.

Using only tear gas, the remaining prison staff regained control of cellblocks B and C, confining over 1,000 inmates to their cells. I remember my father telling us that the gas was so thick in the service tunnels he could barely see five feet in front of himself. He talked about his forearms aching with a pain similar to really bad sunburn. The more he sweated, the more the gas would burn his exposed skin. My mother asked him how his eyes were holding out. He said he knew enough not to rub them, and as long as he let them tear, they would be fine. Dad took a couple more bites of his now half-eaten second sandwich and continued.

The inmates had given up twelve injured guards and civilians to obtain medical help. They still held thirty-eight guards as hostage. After reminding himself of his thirty-eight friends, my father took one last drink of coffee, grabbed two of the packs of cigarettes my mother had left on the dashboard for him, and told us he had to go back in. My mother clasped the back of his head with her hand, gave him a longer than usual kiss, and said, "Be careful, Vance. I love you." My father paused for a second, winked at my mother, and said, "I'll call you." He then got out of the car and walked back into the prison.

The next few days were hell as I am sure they were for all the families of those impacted by the takeover. My mother stayed home from work, but my sister and I were forced to continue going to school. The rumors continued to swirl around us on Friday. The father of one of my friends was a hostage, and my classmate was notably absent from school. It was rumored his father had been castrated. I knew this kid, and he was a friend of mine. I had been to his house and met his father. I couldn't help but be grateful my father was one of the fortunate that was on the outside looking in.

My mother was glued to the television at noon and six o'clock each day where she would quickly click through the available news channels to learn what she could about the riot's progression. If she wasn't watching the news, she was listening to the radio. My sister and I couldn't wait to get home from school. We looked forward to an update on our father and finding out what was actually happening at the prison. To me, my father was bigger than life, and I struggled not to allow myself to entertain thoughts of anything happening to him.

One of the twelve released hostages, a guard named Quinn, was thrown out a third-story window during the initial uprising. By the time he died on Friday, a dozen armed state police had already been added to the contingent of guards. As a result of Quinn's death, prisoners became liable to prosecution for murder. The riot became national news. Commissioner Oswald had offered to accept twenty-eight of thirty prisoner demands. The inmates held out for prisoner amnesty and the firing of Warden Mancusi. As a compromise to their demand for amnesty, Oswald offered the inmates an injunction to prevent retaliation from prison officials. They considered the court injunction worthless and tore it up. Negotiations came to a standstill.

When my father finally made it home for the first time that weekend, we discovered that much of what the media had released to the public was toned down and censored. The conditions at Attica were worse than the public was being led to believe. My father told us about blindfolded hostages being forced into trenches where they were doused with gasoline and threatened to be set on fire. Just before the guards were ordered to stand down, my father heard a hostage cry out, "I don't want to die!"

The state police asked for permission to fire at the inmates holding Molotov cocktails, but permission was never given. These were the stories not covered by the media, the things that only those who were there knew and carried with them. Threatened hostages were eventually allowed to climb out of the trenches and taken back to rejoin their fellow hostages.

Inmates had newsmen film the hostages to show their families they were still alive. I saw people on television I had met—friends of my father. They sat blindfolded on a bench in the D-yard surrounded by inmates wearing football helmets and toting baseball bats. They pleaded for more time and warned against an assault. Sergeant Cunningham laid it out for everyone. "If Rockefeller doesn't come, I'm a dead man."

As the deadline for the end of negotiations approached, inmates began passing the microphone from one to another. They appealed for the governor to come to the prison. Governor Rockefeller was adamant he wasn't coming. By Sunday afternoon, preparations were underway for an assault by state troopers and National Guardsmen. The remaining prison guards had no intentions of standing down.

On Monday morning, an inmate yelled across the DMZ through a megaphone that all hostages would be killed if state troopers tried to recapture the compound. Prison officials demanded immediate release of the hostages. The inmates replied, "Negative." Four hostages were then taken to the central gallery area called "Times Square" where one by one, an inmate jerked their heads back and put a knife to their throats. Other inmates held knives to the throats of the hostages remaining in D-yard. Sharpshooters were advised to take aim at inmates threatening hostages. Prison officials launched plans to undertake an offensive within the hour. Prison guards participated on a volunteer basis, assisting state troopers and National Guardsmen. Sharpshooters took aim from the cellblock roofs.

Two helicopters then flew over the prison, dropping tear gas into D-yard. The drop was immediately followed by an order to "Move in." With a 12-gauge pump shotgun, my father ran down the A-block corridor, across the DMZ, through the prisoner-controlled gates, and across D-yard. Helicopters remained hovering over the D-yard, broadcasting to the inmates through an external speaker. "Put your hands over your head. Walk to the outside of the yard. You will not be harmed. Do not harm the hostages." Gunfire was muffled by the sound of the helicopters.

Those who resisted—inmates throwing spears and Molotov cocktails—were shot. Rescuers tried to reach the captive guards. When it was all said and done, nine hostages and twenty-six inmates had died. The inmates had used the hostages as human shields, and Sergeant Cunningham was dead as he had predicted.

Despite news reports of throats being slit and hostage castrations, pathologists determined all nine of the hostages had died from gunshot wounds. It was further determined through ballistics that not all expelled ammunition could be traced to signed-out armory weapons. Some guns had come from outside the prison. A medical examiner confirmed prisoner accusations that ringleaders had been systematically shot. Families of the deceased inmates filed lawsuits, and many guards, including my father, continued being called to testify in court well into their retirement.

My father's picture appeared in *LIFE* magazine; it was after the taking of D-yard and showed him standing in the yard, still full of dead bodies and smoke. My father did what he had to do to save his friends and be able to live with himself. I doubt I could have put it into words at the time, but even as a teenager,

I knew that life would be different after that. I saw the ugliness of it all, the dead bodies, and the true face of it, as did my father.

Evil is not always an old man sitting on a washing machine, a stranger trying to lead you into the woods, or an invisible spirit ringing a phone on demand. Evil comes in all colors, shapes, and sizes. It looms in the darkness and under stairwells, always ready to pounce on the unsuspecting and unaware. Evil was with us—it seemed to follow the men of our family, perhaps as far back as the recollection. The warnings echoed in my mind. "*Be sober, be vigilant; because your adversary the devil, as a roaring lion, walks about, looking for whom he may devour*" (1 Peter 5:8).

Just as I never asked my father about the time he spent in Korea or my uncle about the concentration camp he liberated during World War II, I never asked my father about the shots he took on the day he helped to liberate Attica's D-yard. My father was a private man, and I knew early in life that a man's burdens are often his alone to carry. Whatever my father may have shared with me, I will take it with me to my grave.

One day while I was at school, the camper was returned to my grandfather. My adventure with the big boys would never happen, and I was at peace with it. My father had personally met evil on September 13 as he had planned. He had shaken hands with the devil, and the price he had to pay was more than any man should ever have to pay.

What was not immediately evident was that a seed had been planted that day. I began to question what was real in a world where I knew that not everything could be seen or understood. Suddenly, the security of my family and routine was not enough. My security blanket had been taken away and burned. There were things in this world I had no control over—things my parents had no control over. I no longer felt safe or protected.

6

THE SABBATICAL

Fall from Grace

By now, the hook had been firmly set. I wanted to breathe above water, to be more than the fish that swam around me. I wanted to do and see things that I was told I shouldn't, to be master of my own world. Rules were meant for the weak and lost, but not for me, or so I thought. What I didn't take into consideration was that my view of the world was skewed and created in a void. I was following in my father's footsteps, down the path of substance abuse and avoidance. I didn't recognize the conflicts in my life, the choices that stared me in the face and begged for a decision. Would I be master of my world, or would my world be master of me? I first would have to find the courage to ask the questions that needed to be asked and then the strength to follow the answers to where they might take me.

Clearly, I needed some time to assess the enormous weight that I felt sitting on my shoulders. I needed to take a breath, to get away from the familiar presence that permeated my life. My father transferred to a medium security prison in Albion, New York, and our family moved a few miles away to a small town called Medina. Being an experienced emergency room nurse, my mother had a job waiting for her at the local hospital. I changed high schools just prior to my senior year, and my sister went off to her first year of college. Though it was never mentioned or realized at the time, we all seemed to be running away from something.

My parents purchased a large, five-bedroom farmhouse in need of repair on the edge of town. There were three large bedrooms and two bathrooms in the front of the upstairs, previously the living quarters, and two smaller bedrooms and a bathroom in the back of the upstairs, which had previously been used as the servant's quarters. I lived in the servant's quarters and had my own private entrance. It was like having my own apartment. When my sister came home from college, she stayed in the front bedroom that adjoined the front hallway and entrance to the servant's quarters. Interestingly, nobody ever used the back stairwell but me.

While my sister and I were well past the age of needing anyone to watch over us, my grandmother Nora was by now a welcome fixture in our home. She occupied a large bedroom off the upstairs hallway, between my parents and my sister. Nora was always reading, seemed to take an interest in just about everything, and could converse with anyone about almost anything. She seldom lost her temper and was the least judgmental person I ever knew. Nora was raised in the Baptist faith, became a Jehovah's Witness, took religious correspondence courses well into her eighties, and eventually settled on The Church of Christ. She read the Bible every night and was a great inspiration to us all.

Unfortunately, my mother was a devout Catholic and unstudied. To my mother, there was no legitimate religion outside of Catholicism. She loved Nora as we all did, but forbade her from discussing her religious beliefs with her children. Looking back on it now, I wonder if that was wise. Nora was obviously the most learned and God-driven of all of us.

It is important to understand the layout of the house and the enormity of it all to fully appreciate the apparitions, voices, and sounds that manifested themselves there. The downstairs had a living room that ran the entire length of the house and was big enough to literally have played catch in. It adjoined a large dining room and an entranceway.

The entranceway provided access to the front door, an enclosed porch and carport, the front stairs, the dining room, and a room that we referred to as the solarium. The solarium had floor-to-ceiling, wall-to-wall windows on the two outside walls. It was furnished with a large player piano, a loveseat, and a chair. The outside walls of windows were well adorned with hanging plants, and potted plants filled the rest of the room, setting on stands, the floor, and the piano.

The kitchen connected with the dining room and the location of the downstairs bathroom. The kitchen also accessed the stairwell to the servant's quarters, a side door, and a backdoor.

The property had two ponds situated on several acres, multiple rose arbors, hedges, paths, a large barn, and an abandoned thirty-foot-deep, round, stone-lined well. The basement contained an enormous octopus furnace with an old mica window on an access door where a person could view the dancing flames of the oil-burning boiler, several rooms, and a six-foot-tall, bottomless cistern filled with black, reflective rainwater.

No matter how much I explored the property, it seemed there was always something new and interesting to discover. When my father and sister first viewed the property, they were told without asking that there would be no moving in early or renting prior to closing. The owners stated they had twice allowed buyers to move in early and both times they had backed out prior to closing. To most people, that would be considered a warning. To my mother, it was probably more like an invitation.

Although my mother had retired the table and my father had long since given up on Blair's Gap, it didn't take long after moving into our new home to see what my mother's attraction to the house had been. Early one morning when Nora was headed down the front stairwell, she looked in the doorway of the solarium and saw a woman dressed in white, sitting in a chair. Nora naturally assumed the woman was a nurse who obviously worked with my mother and was waiting for a ride to work or something. Grandma said good morning, walked into the kitchen, poured a cup of coffee, and sat down in the living room.

A short while later, my mother came down dressed for work and grabbed a cup of coffee from the kitchen. When she sat down in the living room with my grandmother to drink her morning coffee, Nora said something about my mother's friend waiting for her in the solarium. Surprised, my mother said, "There's nobody waiting for me."

They both got up to look in the solarium and saw nobody was there. This was no doubt a surprise to my grandmother and a great disappointment to my mother. Aside from my mother's contact through her table, she never experienced any of the apparitions the rest of the family endured.

While living together in that house, I discovered my father and I had more in common than either one of us would have cared to admit. Though we never recognized it as evil, we shared a desire to be free of apparitions, and with no conscious thought of what we were doing, we turned to substance abuse as a means of coping with the things we couldn't control. I secretly started smoking marijuana at night, and my father continued with his habit of drinking three or four beers each night. That was how we quieted the unwelcome guests.

What we didn't know was that our substance abuse was our weakness, and it held the door open to whatever we were so desperately trying to keep out. As I later learned, evil feeds on weakness, fear, and ignorance. I think perhaps because my mother had raised her children to accept the unusual, my father was more troubled than the rest of us. Whatever presence was there, it recognized my father's uneasiness and seemed to taunt him because of it. He once watched a lady walk up the front stairwell, turn toward him, look him in the eye, smile, and disappear before his eyes.

That was only the beginning of it. Many spirits were seen and heard in that house, even by me. My sister and I appeared to be the most sensitive. I attempted to drown out the background noises by listening to a record player in my room. My sister will tell you that the louder I played my records, the louder the noises became. My bedroom closet adjoined her bedroom closet, and when she was home from school, she would often march over to my room to demand that I stop banging on the closet wall. Eventually, my sister figured out that it wasn't me banging on the closet wall. She closed her closet door and learned to live with the sounds of muffled banging and dragging chains. I never heard the chains, only the banging.

Undaunted by almost anything, Nora seemed to unintentionally attract the most activity. Nora once told my sister that a spirit used to gently rock her bed at night. She said she would just continue to read her Bible and pray and the gentle rocking would eventually lull her to sleep. I look back now with great fondness on all the mornings that she asked me what I was dreaming about the night before. I was apparently laughing so hard in my sleep that I often woke her. I was a happy person who actually did laugh and joke a lot. It wasn't inconceivable that I was also laughing in my sleep; after all, I was quite entertained by myself.

Now that I am nearly sixty, I can remember waking up laughing on several occasions. Sadly, I seldom remembered my dreams from the previous night when my grandmother asked. Then one morning, Nora asked me what I had been laughing about the night before on a night that I hadn't fallen asleep. I said, "I don't think I was laughing last night."

Before I could tell her I was up most of the night, Grandmother said, "Oh, but you were. I walked into your sister's room when I first heard it to make sure it was you. I definitely heard laughter coming from the back of the house." That scared me more than just a little to know that an entity hung out in the servant's quarters always laughing, whether I slept or not.

My mother was the Polish daughter of a woman who once experienced stigmata, a spontaneous issuance of blood from wounds that appear in the palms of her hands and are thought to be symbolic of Christ's wounds on the cross. Her mother twice had a visitation from the Virgin Mary. My mother married the son of a devoutly religious woman, a man whose grandfather was a preacher and the source of the recollection.

Perhaps because of her Catholic heritage, perhaps because of her work as an emergency room nurse, my mother struggled with questions of life and death, light and darkness, things seen and unseen. Long after I moved out, my mother confessed to my sister she was puzzled by the fact that she had been the only one not to have witnessed apparitions in the house on Salt Works Road. She seemed disappointed. It's funny how life turns out. My mother seemed to be the only one who *wanted* to experience a haunting, and she never found what she was looking for. Everyone else wanted nothing to do with familiar spirits, and we all had our fill of them.

I thought long and hard about what my mother had told my sister. I was well into my fifties and long past my mother's passing when the pieces finally came together for me. Why had she been the only one who hadn't witnessed apparitions in the house on Salt Works Road? To answer that question, I first needed to consider some additional variables. Yes, she was the heart and soul behind the table, but why wasn't she able to run it by herself? Why did my sister or I have to be there with her? For that matter, why had she encouraged us to operate the Ouija board by ourselves?

One day it clicked—all the pieces fell into place for me. It was my sister and I who had opened the doors to the entities in the house on Salt Works Road. It had always been us. I had opened the door to Alfreido and Blair's Gap. We didn't do these things intentionally, but rather, they happened because we believed they could. Our mother taught us from day one that all things were possible if we only opened our minds. We believed her and approached life accordingly.

At some point, my mother secretly went for a private reading with a woman who read tarot cards. The woman told her that her house was haunted and that she needed to put a rosary in every room for protection. Living in a haunted house was a badge of honor for her. Among my mother's coworkers at the hospital, the haunted house was the talk of the town. Friends that my parents had known since before my mother's séances were not surprised.

After my mother's visit to the tarot reader, she placed a rosary in every room and hung them on nearly every curtain rod, but I never noticed. She was a member of the Holy Rosary Society and it didn't seem at all odd to see rosaries lying around the house. Sometime later, when my sister was playing the piano, a rosary that my mother had placed on the piano flew off the piano and across the room. I was glad that I hadn't been home to witness that. Most people who had spent a single night in that house confessed to hearing muffled voices and strange noises. There were many places in that house that I simply wouldn't go in if I were alone. Although no word was ever spoken of it, everyone but my mother seemed to feel the same uneasiness.

I lived in the haunted house my entire senior year. After high school, I went to work in Medina at the Bernz-O-Matic plant, unloading propane torches from the brazing furnace. I had only been working there for a few months when the plant temporarily closed for remodeling and expansion. It gave me a chance to think about what I really wanted to do with my life.

One thing I knew for sure, my life wasn't normal and nothing like the lives of my friends. I decided to follow in my father's example. He was a Korean War veteran who had enlisted in the service and left home at the age of seventeen. He was bigger than life to me. I was born in October and graduated high school at the age of seventeen. I was ready to make my mark in the world and hoped that the Vietnam War wouldn't be over before I got a chance to get over there and see what it was all about.

The lottery draft system was in effect when I announced to my father that I was enlisting in the service and asked him for a ride down to the recruiter's office. I wanted to join the Marines, and my father did everything in his power to discourage me. He told me that if he were a young man and had life to do over, he would join the Navy and see the world. Fortunately, the Marine recruiters were out to lunch when I arrived, so I went across the hall to waste some time with the Navy. Two hours later, I had joined the Navy and was headed off to see the world.

By the time I got out of boot camp, the United States had ceased deploying troops and was conducting massive withdrawals. I was thankful for my father's advice. Even though I wasn't shipping off to Vietnam, I was at least heading off to see the world. To me, seeing the world meant seeing what I had missed, a fresh start, turning the recollection of Blair's Gap and the house on Salt Works Road into a small dot in my rearview mirror.

To most people that might sound like I was running away, but it wasn't at all. I wanted to fill the blackboard with chalk dust to dilute the memories I stored in an ocean of memorable recollections. I wanted to see, experience, and taste everything. I wanted to breathe above water, to taste the forbidden fruit.

One thing was certain, I had experienced more than most by the time I turned seventeen. Either the familiar spirits I had heard and seen in my youth were real, or I was insane. Therefore, I believed the demons were real because I would not entertain thoughts of insanity, which were thoughts devoid of hope.

Newton's third Universal Law of Motion tells us that for every action, there is an equal and opposite reaction; there is no Ying without a Yang. Certainly, if I am to acknowledge that familiar spirits and pure evil exist, I must also acknowledge that angels and an Almighty God exist—a dangerous concept that is not without serious consequence.

If God is real, then His Word is real, and if His Word is real, there will be judgment and who can stand against God's judgment? As it is written, "*A man also, or woman, that hath a familiar spirit, or that is a wizard, shall surely be put to death: they shall stone them with stones; their blood shall be upon them*" *(Leviticus 20:27)*. I looked to my final judgment and found I hadn't a leg to stand on.

I read carefully the warning of the prophet Isaiah to the virgin daughter of Babylon: "*Stand now with your enchantments and with the multitude of your sorceries, wherein you have labored since your youth. You are exhausted in the multitude of your counsels. Let now the astrologers, the stargazers, the monthly prognosticators, stand up and save you from these things that shall come upon you. Behold, they shall be as stubble: the fire shall burn them; they shall not deliver themselves from the power of the flame: there shall not be a coal to warm at or a fire that you might sit before*" (Isaiah

47:12–14). For the first time, I felt as though my soul was in jeopardy.

At seventeen, I may have seemed more self-aware than my peers, and maybe I was; I was identified early as having a higher than average aptitude. All I knew was that my life was not like everyone else's, and I was going to correct that, right or wrong. I was out of there. I was going to be a Gunner's Technician–Bombs.

In Nuclear Weapons School, I became lifelong friends with a classmate named John. He was a few years older than me and had seen and done many things in life that I thought I had missed out on. He had dark wavy hair, wore blue-tinted glasses, and had an attractive, young hippie wife named Judy. John drove a Chevy van that sported the KEEP ON TRUCKIN' logo and cartoon character painted on both sides. He was a Navy veteran of Vietnam who had been honorably discharged, fallen in love, gotten married, and reenlisted. We hit it off right away.

John and I shipped off to the USS Oriskany, CVA-34. We were qualified dealers of death and destruction. On the boat, we made friends with a fellow GMT named Dennis. Dennis was about five foot, four inches tall. He had rusty red hair, blue eyes, and a stocky build. He was a real ladies' man and a good guy to be friends with. Dennis had already been on the boat for a couple of years by the time John and I arrived. He seemed to size people up pretty quickly. After talking with us for about a half an hour, Dennis invited us to go walk around the base and smoke a joint. John and I couldn't help but like him.

After we smoked that joint, John took off somewhere, and Dennis and I went back to the boat. We were hanging out, talking, and getting to know each other on one of the catwalks that overlooked the base. I was curious about Dennis and asked him if he had a special girl back home that he still thought about.

Dennis said he did and that she lived in his hometown of Dayton, Ohio. I asked him if she was a cute little blonde, and he said that she was. I asked him if his car played a special part in their relationship. Dennis smiled and said that it did. He had a Volkswagen Beetle. Every time I asked Dennis a question, the answer was always the same—yes.

Then out of the blue, I told Dennis he had a Volkswagen convertible and used to slide the roof back so his girlfriend could sit on his lap. Without realizing it, I was giving Dennis a reading. This went on for about twenty minutes. Dennis seemed amused by our conversation, but I needed to stop. I needed to break away from the easy and familiar. The abilities that my mother had crafted in me would never be a dot in my rearview mirror if I didn't first find the strength to drive past them.

If I was going to break free, I needed to immerse myself in the world, to go deep and experience it all. I needed to find a world so far from what I was accustomed to that I might never find my way back to those things that I so deeply wanted to forget. My ability to know things and my familiarity with spirits were still fresh in my mind. I hadn't yet jumped into the deep end of the pool.

Still, I couldn't help but wonder where the information about Dennis had come from. Was it the same small voice that told me when the television would be repaired? I again made a concerted effort to block out the thought of any perceived or imagined psychic ability. I wanted nothing to do with it. I was changing my inner dialogue, experiencing new things, and defining a new world. It was what I needed to do to survive, to hide the unwanted variables in a maze of unrelated equations.

Dennis took me under his wing and made the Navy an enjoyable experience for me. We had been out to sea for a couple of weeks when Dennis invited me to take a walk with him. I followed him through a deck hatch and down a flight of stairs to a storeroom where I first met Warren. Warren was a tall, lanky guy, all stretched out on a comfortable civilian couch, wearing headphones and listening to a stereo when we walked in. He smiled as we stepped over the knee knocker, the lower knife-edge of the watertight integrity-door, took off his headphones, and stood up as I was introduced.

Dennis and Warren were obviously good friends and joked around with one another for a few minutes. Warren had a coworker, but that was the only time I met him, and five minutes later, I forgot his name. After sizing each other up for ten or fifteen minutes, Warren shut off his stereo, and Dennis and I followed him and his coworker out of the hatch. Warren dogged the door behind us and padlocked it.

We probably followed him down ten levels of steel, mezzanine stairwell to a storeroom where the ship's soap supply was kept. Warren unlocked the padlocked hatch, swung open the dogs—the levers along the edge of the hatch to ensure that it is watertight—and opened the hatch. As I stepped over the knee-knocker, Warren turned and told me to dog—re-latch—the door behind us. When I dogged the last dog, I realized there was no place on the bulkhead to secure the dogging bar, which is a hollow pipe used for leverage to secure dogs, so I left it on the last dog. The four of us sat down on pallets of laundry soap. Dennis told me that the soap absorbed the smell of marijuana. Then Warren pulled out a joint from his shirt pocket and lit it up.

I was getting very, very stoned. The joint had made it around a few times before someone ate the roach and Warren lit another. Just as the second joint was being passed to me for the first time, somebody whispered, "Shh . . . I think I hear something." I grabbed the joint, and then I heard it too. I heard the clanging of someone's steps coming down the steel mezzanine stairwell. I now had to hang on to the joint. It was like musical chairs, and I lost; nobody wanted it now. It took whoever it was about a minute to make it down the stairs.

Whoever it was never said a word. He just started undogging the door from the outside. He had two or three dogs undogged when he came to the dog that I had left the dogging bar on. The dogging bar swung around and hit a support in the bulkhead. He couldn't open the door from the outside. Everyone's mouths fell open; nobody could believe our luck. Dennis signaled for me to eat the joint, so I tossed it in my mouth. The visitor slammed the dogging bar against the bulkhead two or three times, knocked on the door a couple of times with no response, and then climbed the stairs.

We waited about five minutes before we swiftly tiptoed back up the stairs. At someone's suggestion, we all split up and left in different directions. After wandering aimlessly around the ship for about an hour, I ran into Dennis again. He was heading back to the berthing compartment and suggested I follow him. That would have been enough for most people to straighten up and fly straight, but not for us.

By now, John had landed himself a second job on the boat. He was one of the ship's disc jockeys, had a room full of albums, and played whatever he wanted over the ship's intercom system most evenings until 9:00 or 10:00 p.m. at night. When people tell you that being on an aircraft carrier is like living in a big city, they're talking about the number of people on the boat, not the number of things available to do in the evening. Landing a job as a ship's disk jockey was a big deal.

Once your work was complete and after you'd eaten, there really wasn't that much to do. Fortunately, we had a couple of amateur guitar players in our department. On occasion, a few of us would gather around the forward magazine locker area and listen to or play the guitar. Somehow between flight ops, on replenishments, and weapons maintenance, we managed to endure the long hours at sea.

In port, all rules flew out the window and anything went as long as you didn't miss the ship's movement. If the lack of rules wasn't enough to get a man in trouble already, in most third-world countries, a single man with a paycheck and no bills might as well have been a millionaire at an amusement park. Almost anything was possible, and almost anyone could be bribed—not a good recipe for a bunch of rowdy sailors who may have been out to sea for as long as nine months. I caught on quickly and became one of the worst offenders. Beer and girls were cheap, and I was carried back to the boat more times than I can remember.

My new lifestyle was not without risk. After Subic, the next port was Hong Kong. As always, before anyone was allowed to go ashore, we were first read the riot act and reminded of the places that were off limits. I listened closely. John had already been on several cruises and seen the seedy side of town so he took off to snap some pictures of the Great Wall of China. I wanted to see the rooftop district, the area we were told to stay away from.

I met a cute little Chinese girl who spoke very good broken English at the first bar I came to. After a couple drinks, she invited me back to her place. She then excused herself to change her clothes and told me she would be back in ten or fifteen minutes. She left her purse on the table. It was open and her money was clearly visible. Surely this cute little girl was not going to roll me in the alley and slit my throat. She had a way of putting me at ease. After about five minutes, the waiter brought me over another drink and apologized for the girl. She'd be about another ten minutes or so and paid for me to have another drink while I waited. Now I was convinced. I must have found the nicest girl in all of China.

I drank a couple of sips of my drink and lit a cigarette. As I reached for my drink a second time, I suddenly felt lightheaded and warm. I stood up, took two steps, and collapsed on the floor. I knew instantly the girl had drugged me. I was completely conscious and aware of my surroundings but unable to move. I could see my date and two Chinese men gathering in the back hall and looking at me. My next stop would surely be the back alley.

Just then, the military police came in the front door. They made a few comments about how intoxicated I must be, picked me up off the floor by my armpits, and walked me back to their jeep. I didn't care how drunk they thought I was, I was glad to get out of there. By the time we made it back to the harbor, I started to come around. I staggered back to the ferry that would take me to my boat and called it a night.

Somewhere in my fog, after completing my first Western Pacific cruise, I met a woman in Berkeley, California, who was just like me. She loved sex, drugs, booze, and good music, pretty much in that order. More importantly, she was attempting to put a portion of her youth in her rearview mirror. I looked at her and saw myself. Both of us thought we should always be the last ones standing and most times we were. I loved her right off the bat and knew instantly I might never again find anyone more capable of understanding me.

We were married two weeks later and heading off to enjoy a year of shore duty in the Philippines. We had access to some of the strongest locally grown marijuana in the world; San Miguel Beer at $3.00 a case; brown Hong Kong Rock heroin; and a small bit of cocaine that we smuggled into the country for special occasions. Coworkers brought their wives to our place in the Mabayuan, and people I knew from town stopped by, along with others when their ship was in port. Every night was a party.

That lasted for about ten months until I had to abruptly move one night because I was informed by someone who knew that the police held a search warrant for my house dated for the next day. Through a friend, I was able to rent the house of a retired police officer, one of very few civilians allowed to own a gun. From that time on, I lived in a home at the top of a hill with no road access and a twenty-four-hour hour armed guard.

The move made my wife nervous. She was afraid I would end up in a Philippine prison and went back to the States to wait for me. I stayed behind, taught my bodyguards how to make marijuana brownies, and managed to stay out of trouble until I went home two months later.

My next duty station was on a tugboat out of Treasure Island, California, which meant that my wife and I would be able to stay in the Bay area. We eventually got an apartment in El Cerrito, and the party continued from there. Both of us knew that we were living a self-destructive lifestyle that would end badly, but it didn't much matter until we started talking about having children.

To me, that meant cleaning up my act, going drug free, and falling into line with the rest of the world. To her, it meant slowing down and staying as free from as many culturally endorsed black-and-white measures of acceptance as possible.

Just as we had a million reasons why we should be together, there were as many reasons why we shouldn't. I like to think that her fear of raising children with me was the reason for our final split. Similar to most facets of our lives, our disagreements were intense, usually short-lived, and sometimes involved flying silverware. Our divorce papers labeled it "irreconcilable differences." Looking back on it now, I see it was probably not a good idea to mix fire with fire, but it was a few good years and I wouldn't trade them for anything.

By the time I got out of the service, Mother's table, the recollection, Blair's Gap, and the house on Salt Works Road were all distant dots in my rearview mirror. The new person I had become no longer called on or even thought much about the powers that previously overwhelmed the old David. Such thoughts seemed to be a part of someone else's past.

My unwanted variables were buried in an abundance of unrelated equations. I had had eleven Captain's Masts, been busted in rank and/or put on restriction more times than I could care to remember, experienced every drug then known to man, and battled addiction with a few of them. I had been with more women by the time I was twenty than most men will know in a lifetime. I had firsthand stories about things that many people would only dream of and others would write about. Unlocking my spirit had come at a cost and with much unanticipated baggage.

Following the fulfillment of my enlistment and an honorable discharge, I went to work as a business and residential phone installer in Berkeley, California. Though only vaguely aware of it at the time, the "in-your-face" demons of my past had become the stealthier, more subtle devils known as cocaine, marijuana, and psilocybin. What I had once used to control my pain had now started to control me.

Fortunately, a recurring anti-cocaine commercial aired on television at the time that began to hit home. The commercial featured a man with a rolled-up hundred-dollar bill snorting a boat, a car, an expensive television, and finally a bank up his nose. Every time I saw it, I recounted how much money I had spent on cocaine in the last few days, and it always came up to be enough to buy that expensive television or stereo.

My addictions started with alcohol. It was easy in the service where everyone drank to excess, beer was three dollars a case, and the alcoholic content of San Miguel beer was over seven percent. Unlike my father, God and Mother Nature worked together to save me from a life of alcohol abuse. Sometime well into my first cruise, I caught what I assumed to be a case of gonorrhea, but turned out to be non-specific urethritis (NSU). The symptoms are much the same, except NSU has no cure and always waits dormant to strike again. The symptoms are excruciating. You always feel like you have to urinate, and when you do, it is like pulling a string of hot razor blades through your urethra.

I learned from my doctor that the NSU was more than likely the result of a life of excesses and could easily be retriggered by something as simple as the hops in my beer or the creamer in my coffee. I immediately switched over to drinking my coffee black. The beer became an unforgiving taskmaster. I discovered through trial and error that I could go out drinking if I wanted to, just not for three days at a time. Every time I went on a three-day bender, I woke up with NSU.

The treatment was truly worse than the disease. It consisted of mega-doses of tetracycline, which in turn caused dehydration and resulted in having to drink five gallons of water a day. At a time when urinating was the last thing I wanted to do, the extra five gallons of water kept a steady stream of razor blades flowing through my urethra. I learned quickly to get my drinking under control.

One Friday night after work, I went with a friend to Hayward, California, where we purchased a few grams of cocaine from a connection before heading over to the house of a mutual friend who also lived in Hayward. The three of us stayed up all night and most of the next day doing lines of coke every hour or so. It was Saturday evening when we finally ran out of cocaine and headed home. Normally, that would have been just another lost weekend that I would fondly remember as a heck of a party, but it wasn't over.

Bright and early the next morning, even before I had a cup of coffee or anything to eat, my buddies from the night before showed up at my doorstep with more cocaine. That was the moment of truth. I knew what I did in the next few minutes would determine the course of my life. If I did one more line it would be the end of me. I was heading down a road I could no longer manage. I knew the cocaine would come out shortly and someone would soon be chopping up lines. I didn't have much time. If I saw the coke I would surely do it. I went to the backyard to think.

Before I knew it, I found myself climbing the eight-foot wooden fence behind my house that led to the parking lot of the gas station on the next street over. I walked down the street ten or fifteen blocks, bought a pack of cigarettes, turned around, and walked back to my house. I knew no one would be waiting for me, and by the time I returned, the cocaine would be long gone. Thankfully, the guys had left and taken the cocaine with them. Every cokehead knows the number of people present is directly proportional to the amount of coke per person. That was the day I turned my back on the cocaine devil, but I missed him for the next ten years. That is the nature of the beast; he always tries to lure you back.

It was clear to me I needed to take a timeout for detoxification and cleansing. I needed to wring myself out and reevaluate my life. I had achieved the dilution and numbness I had so desperately been seeking, but what was next? Where did I intend to go from there, and what did I hope to accomplish? I had no idea. I hadn't thought that far ahead. One thing was for sure, it seemed destructive to stay where I was. My friends were prostitutes, junkies, and cokeheads. They were heading down a slippery slope to the point of disaster and no return. I chewed on that thought for a few days and decided my best bet was to move back east, again away from the easy and familiar, away from my friends and connections.

I was entitled to GI Bill benefits, grants, and student loans. I could make a decent living going to college, at least for a few years, until I figured out what I wanted to do next. Within a few weeks of turning my back on the cocaine devil, I quit my job with the phone company and moved back east to attend college on my GI Bill. Minus a few changes of clothes, I left everything I owned in California. There was no time to be sentimental. I was reinventing myself again. Still, there were unseen forces working against me, forces that would inevitably wipe the slate clean and bring the recollection, Blair's Gap, and the appointment back into focus.

7

REAFFIRMATION

The Reminder

Once I enlisted in the Navy, contact with my family was at best sketchy. Following boot camp, I next saw my parents four years later after I had completed my enlistment and was working for the phone company in Berkeley, California. My parents and I absolutely loved each other, but I was trying to discover myself and come to terms with what I referred to as my unique upbringing. I was more comfortable with the black-and-white, three-dimensional worlds in which most people lived than the shades of gray, multi-dimensional world I grew up in. It was easier to pretend psychic abilities and spiritual forces of evil didn't exist than to deal with them. Besides, there was a lot in the earthly world I hadn't yet seen or experienced.

My sister Patricia took a different path in her life. Rather than running away from her unique childhood, I felt as though she embraced it. I might have seen her once and spoken with her maybe three times in the six years between enlisting in the Navy, getting married, getting divorced, and moving back east.

Patricia was in her first year of college when I enlisted and working in New Jersey as a research chemist when I moved back to New York. The first time I spoke with her in any depth was when our mother was dying of lung cancer. She took vacation to spend time with our mother before she passed, and afterward, she stayed on to spend time with our father. Needless to say, our minds were on other things, more important things, like learning how to cope with the loss of our mother. We never discussed our upbringing or how it had affected us.

Eight months later, I began to learn a bit about my sister's interests and personal life. While I had spent the last six years trying to suppress and deny my so-called "abilities," my sister had been trying to expand and develop hers. A couple of years earlier while having her tarot cards read, the medium asked my sister if she would like to learn more at a class that was being held that evening. Growing up with visits to Lilly Dale and in-home séances, how could my sister resist?

In her words, she was developing her gifts and exploring her spiritualism. She began studying under a well-known psychic couple from New Jersey. She told me she was planning a trip to Blair's Gap with some psychic friends and wanted our father to go along. I didn't know what to say. Blair's Gap was the very last place I wanted to think about.

Although my father is no longer alive to verify it, I am sure the sheer notion of a trip to Blair's Gap had a completely different meaning for my sister than it did for my father and me. My sister saw it as just another chance to possibly experience psychic phenomenon. For me, thoughts of Blair's Gap brought vivid memories of the appointment made so many years earlier at my mother's séance in Ohio and the events surrounding it, the old man sitting on the washer, and the confirmation of evil. It was probably worse for my father who had a personal connection between Blair's Gap and the Attica riot.

I wished my sister hadn't forced me to remember the appointment. I hoped she wouldn't go and resented her for trying to make it happen. Whether my father was still under the influence of the appointment or simply working to be supportive of my sister after our mother's passing, I didn't know, but it looked like he was going. And as much as I didn't like to entertain the thought of it, if my father was going to Blair's Gap, I was going to Blair's Gap.

I took the idea of our trip seriously and approached it with much trepidation. Playing with evil was not something I took lightly or thought of as fun. In my opinion, I felt as though my sister looked forward to the opportunity of standing close to the flames. I thought that perhaps if she had been burnt a few times, she might stand back a little further as I intended to do.

It bothered me that she had put herself in the middle of something so intense and life changing for my father and me. After all, she wasn't even in Ohio when the appointment was made. She hadn't seen the old man or spoke with her grandfather. She wasn't even there when I found the stone. I never considered myself as being sanctimonious, but what we were intending to do felt sacrilegious, like drinking Wild Turkey in church. I felt as though we were not approaching the trip to Blair's Gap with the level of respect it demanded, like we were going to fight Mohammed Ali with kid gloves.

Although I hadn't had all the psychic training my sister had, and I might never fully understand her motives, I eventually accepted we were going and got over being upset with her. I lulled myself into a false sense of security in knowing that we were not going to speak with the traveler. We were simply going to witness or be part of some unrelated psychic phenomenon. My father and I had already missed our appointment at Blair's Gap. Our once burning desire had now been suppressed for nearly ten years, and it was clear that without Patricia's pushing, neither one of us would be making the trip on our own anytime soon.

I began to think of our upcoming weekend as a sort of scavenger hunt. At the very least, it would be a family camping trip, something I would enjoy and remember. I looked forward to spending time with my father and sister who now lived several hours away from me.

Although I can't speak for my father, I can tell you that as I rationalized our trip to Blair's Gap, I didn't anticipate anything significant happening that weekend. I figured we would simply drive around for four or five hours, maybe or maybe not find Blair's Gap, and eventually drive back to the campsite disappointed.

After all, it had been nearly ten years since the appointment was missed, and the appointment had been between my father, Dick, and the traveler. We were going with nine people and a big Labrador Retriever named Ozzie: my sister and her boyfriend Jim; friends of Patricia's and Jim's, Terry and Ginger; Patricia's paranormal guide Art and his wife Vicky; me and my girlfriend Ann; and my father. I couldn't admit it to myself at the time, but something was pulling me to Blair's Gap. Perhaps my sister and father felt the same thing.

It was obvious Patricia had done her homework. She had talked with Nora extensively over the phone and corresponded with her in great detail about the actual location of Blair's Gap. With Nora's help, my sister had made a hand-drawn map we intended to use as a guide on our trip.

By this time, it had been over seventy years since the recollection, and I expected many of the landmarks would have changed. Blacktop roads would have replaced abandoned logging roads, and forests would have been cleared for farming and new construction. If we were going to find Blair's Gap, it would take my sister's map and my father's childhood memories to get us there. My sister made arrangements for all of us to meet at our Great-Aunt Midge's house in Marienville, Pennsylvania, on Friday, August 13, 1982.

When Ann and I pulled in the driveway, everyone else had already arrived. Midge was Nora's sister and just as much a part of the recollection as Nora was. She was happy to support us in our little adventure and looked forward to hearing what, if anything, we might discover.

Midge's house sat on the edge of town, the very last house on the paved road. Just below her house, the paved road turned into a dirt road that went back into the forest and had many campsites. Because Midge's house was a small, two-bedroom A-frame and we didn't want to impose, it was decided beforehand that we would all be camping in the forest that weekend, somewhere below Midge's house. We would set up camp there that night and set out on our search the next morning.

After getting acquainted with everyone, we all drove down to scope out possible campsites and found a nice location about three miles into the woods. We had a nice stone ring set up for campfires, lots of dead wood around for the actual fire, a spring and running stream across the road, and maybe even a picnic table as I remember. Patricia had definitely done her homework.

We started a fire, cooked some wieners, and drank some beer while we discussed our plans for the next day. Looking at my sister's map, Art was the first to notice that Highway 666 intersected with Highway 13 in the forest. These highways only ran in the forest and appeared to be the two main arteries. Art stated that these were unusual numbers for highways because the number 666 is usually attributed to the beast in the book of Revelations, and the number 13 has always been considered unlucky.

Once everyone had a chance to take a look at the map and taking into account the very few noted landmarks, everyone agreed our best starting point would be to see if we could locate a place known as Crystal Springs. Crystal Springs was somewhere south on Highway 13 and would first require that we find Highway 666. In order to find Highway 666, we would first have to drive down the dirt road by Big Salmon Creek, the same road our campsite was located on.

It sounded like we had a plan, so Ann and I made ourselves scarce at that point. We were both sleeping in the open bed of my pickup truck and headed off to see if we could find somewhere more private to park for the night. Not having experienced all the psychic training that my sister had and perhaps because I had taken a different path in life, I really didn't put much stock in all the other worldly things that the group was discussing. Besides, I had decided long before we left that I would approach this trip as an observer rather than a participant. I was standing back from the flames for fear of being burned. Still, something drove me to want to come along. We went to the Guitonville family cemetery to park for the night.

When Ann and I returned the next morning, we barely had time to brush our teeth at the spring. Everyone had already eaten breakfast and was in the process of breaking camp. Even the car arrangements had already been made. Being the most familiar with the area, my father rode in the backseat of the lead car with my sister and his dog Ozzie.

Following Nora's hand-drawn map, my sister gave directions from the backseat. Art drove the lead car, and Vicky rode shotgun with the green-eyed stone of protection to "channel" psychic indicators and warnings. Terry and Ginger followed the lead car with their own car, and Jim rode in the back. Ann and I brought up the rear with my old Toyota pickup truck. Patricia's car and my father's car were left at the campsite. It looked like we were finally on our way.

Between leaving the night before and returning in the morning, the group had apparently drunk all the beer and altered the plan just a tiny bit. Before we began our search, we would first have to stop by Marienville to replenish the beer and ice.

On the way to the outlet store, Vicky reported hearing the voice of a man in his fifties telling her to be careful. He apparently told her to protect herself and that he would not be contacting her again. My sister's intuitive response was it had to be our grandfather speaking. He was the person who had initially told my father he would be sending him the stone for protection some ten years previous.

After obtaining the necessary ice and beer, we headed back past the campsite, along Big Salmon Creek. On the drive, Vicky reported hearing several additional voices at different times; all were telling her to be careful. One voice in particular was the voice of a little girl who told her she would be with her throughout the entire day if she were needed.

Ever cynical, I assumed my father must have been biting his lip. He, however, never spoke a word of skepticism, quietly participated, and was respectful of my sister's friends. Ann and I thought Art and Vicky were a little too far from center to be taken seriously. I know if my girlfriend Ann and I had been in the lead car and heard Vicky describing the voices she heard, we would have found it hard to maintain our composure. Regardless of any perceived entertainment value we may have found in Vicky, my sister appeared slightly nervous. She said, "Something will surely happen with so many warnings coming through."

As a more mature adult and a shameless follower of Jesus Christ now, I know what it is to be the only one in a crowded room with a conflicting belief that represents their truth. I have been in many heated, closed-door meetings where the voice of reason fought to be heard and was lost. In hindsight, it took a lot of courage for my sister to let my father and I join her merry band on this quest for psychic discovery and enlightenment. She had left herself wide open to ridicule and embarrassment by bringing us along. And in some small way, I regrettably took the bait. I say that because fear of ridicule and embarrassment may well have contributed to my own escape into a world of self-indulgence and drug abuse.

Shortly after we turned west onto Highway 666, we passed a couple stretches of forest that brought my sister to attention. As she recalled, they sent chills up and down her spine and made the hair stand up on her arms. Art commented the woods looked like the Black Forest of Germany. Patricia described them as being dark and menacing, even in full sunlight. Each time we drove past one of these menacing sections, Art would speed up. The conversation would all but die off in the lead car until they had passed by the offending sections of forest. Ann and I were driving so fast to keep up with the rest of the caravan that we barely noticed the Black Forest.

One thing we had all noticed was that after we had turned onto Highway 666 West, we never again saw a highway sign that read "666 West"; they simply read, "West." Art and Vicky felt this was not at all unusual. Art said people were told to leave and only the right people would be able to find their way without the signs.

Back in the truck, Ann and I came up with our own explanation. I figured the signs were like the signs on the corner of Haight and Ashbury in San Francisco. Every time the city replaced them, they were again immediately stolen as souvenirs by wannabe hippies. The state probably got tired of continually replacing the signs. After all, what "gothic" high school student, dabbler in the dark arts, or skull-loving motorcycle enthusiast wouldn't enjoy a 666, "Mark of the Beast" sign in their garage?

Prior to locating Highway 13, the lead car had passed a particularly dark and menacing section of forest they wished to return to and explore after they found Crystal Springs. Unknown to the lead car, Jim had simultaneously noted the exact same section of the forest from the second car and commented that he wished Art would stop there on the way back.

Later, Jim told Patricia that when riding past that section of forest, he had become nauseous. Patricia was keeping a log of our adventure and noted, "It was unfortunate we had to use so many vehicles and that all the various impressions could not be gathered at once, but would rather have to be pieced together later."

After a while, we passed by an unmarked side road. Everyone in the lead car looked behind them to see if they might have missed a road sign or if there might be a road sign from the other direction, but nobody saw any markers or signs. We were all expecting Highway 13 to be clearly marked since it was one of only two major highways that ran through the forest.

Later, the lead car realized the side road must have been Highway 13, and we all turned around. When we approached from the opposite direction, we all saw a sign that clearly read, "Road to Tionesta". That was the one. Going south on Highway 13, there were no signs indicating it was actually Highway 13 for the entire length of the highway. I again attributed the lack of signs to souvenir hunters. The number 13 was the universally accepted symbol for marijuana and bad luck. What college student, wannabe hippie, or down-on-his-luck gambler wouldn't want one? Although I don't know it to be true, I would assume Art and Vicky were sticking to their story about only the right people being able to find their way without signs.

We were lucky Nora had provided us with a good map containing all the available landmarks and twists and turns in the road. Finally, we stopped at Crystal Springs. There were no houses, just a turn in the road to mark the spot. We all pulled over to the side of the road, and Art began to unload his cameras and electronic equipment. My sister had an itinerary that apparently included a stop at Crystal Springs. Two hours down the road, and we finally found our starting point.

For some unknown reason and without saying a word, we all seemed to walk about fifteen feet into the woods and gravitate toward the same dead tree. From this point forward, Patricia, Jim, Art, and Vicky took pictures throughout the entire day. The tree was lying on its side and looked like a large, old, rotten pine box, having all its limbs broken off, sharp and dangerous like spikes.

As Art began to explain how his equipment would work, Vicky and Jim each took off in opposite directions into the woods. Patricia felt they each had been drawn into the woods by "something different." Everyone else stayed to hear what Art had to say. He decided he wanted to turn his tape recorder on to see if he could pick up any strange sounds near the dead tree. We all tried to be silent as we listened, but the sound of an occasional car driving by just twenty feet away made it hard to concentrate.

Patricia thought she could hear some kind of chanting, like a ritual. When she closed her eyes, she could see a line of people in white robes, following a leader who carried a wooden symbol of some sort. Just as Patricia began to tell Art about this, Vicky returned from a small creek saying that she had been "picking up" some sort of chanting. The rest of us heard nothing at all unusual. When the tape was played back, there definitely was something there, something hard to make out, but there. Art's guess was that it was several voices, each talking one over the other.

Art said the spot we were standing on had been used for both good and bad. It was a natural power center, and rituals had been performed there. I wondered why Art had chosen the term "good and bad" rather than "good and evil" as I would have expected. I wasn't sure if I was blocking obvious phenomena or taking part in some sort of group hysteria. If I had my druthers, I'd rather think of it as some sort of group hysteria where everyone was feeding off everyone else.

That was how our day began. We made two or three such stops that morning before finally searching out Blair's Gap. Not much to show for our efforts, we wound up with a couple of rocks in Art's trunk, several pictures, and some questionable audio recordings.

Because we had spent so much time at Crystal Springs, we were now running a little later than anticipated. Even though several of us were rather hungry by that time, everyone wanted to get to Blair's Gap before nightfall. We all agreed we would wait until we got back to the campsite that night to eat. Again, we were looking for a dirt road that had no clear markings. After a few wrong turns and couple of false starts, we finally felt as though we were on the right road and nearing the end of our quest.

Patricia noted Vicky's complexion grew paler and paler as they made it further and further down the road. Vicky gripped my father's green-eyed rock so tightly her fingertips and knuckles turned white. She looked down at the rock and exclaimed that, "The green eyes are glowing!"

My sister then leaned forward and looked at the rock in Vicky's lap. Patricia said she could see some flickering of green light. Seemingly disappointed at what Patricia had said, Vicky commented, "The lights are getting dimmer."

As Patricia sat back in her seat, my father asked if they were on the right road. "Maybe we should turn around," he said. Without hesitation and based solely on Vicky's reaction, Patricia said, "No. We're headed in the right direction."

Patricia felt our father subconsciously wanted to turn around because he knew we were headed in the right direction. In my sister's words, he felt uncomfortable going back to a place he had tried so hard to avoid, a menacing place made scarier by the uncontrolled and unspoken thoughts that were allowed to feed on one another unchecked for ten years. It was a place that had taken an identity of its own, a place associated with the evil and death that my father had experienced in the retaking of the Attica D-yard.

As we got closer to Blair's Gap, Vicky began acting anxious, like someone having a panic attack. Then out of the blue, she blurted, "It will be about a mile up the road now." Art's odometer wasn't working, but he agreed and nodded his head up and down. As we approached a turn in the road, both Art and Vicky together said, "That's the place." Art then began to pull the lead car over to the side of the road and everyone in unison said, "It's over on the left."

The caravan pulled over and everyone got out of the vehicles. Art commented it was interesting he had driven over ten hours to get there, and in the end, it was a small rock that had led us to the spot we were looking for. Vicky then said something about how the rock had been glowing.

Still not convinced, I immediately thought the sunlight must have shown through one of the windows and reflected off the rock. Art walked over to the side of the road, looked around, and said, "This is the spot. The rocks are here and everything is where it should be. Patricia, bring the salt."

The spot where we stopped was considerably different than Crystal Springs and the menacing section of woods we referred to as the Black Forest. It was late in the afternoon on a day that had been hot and sticky, and the black flies and mosquitoes were thick. It was the first time we had seen or been bothered by any insects all day.

The edge of the forest sloped down to a rock-cluttered gully that ran parallel to the road and seemed to draw us toward it. Brier bushes and prickly things grew in the forest and all along the edge of the gully. The floor of the gully was carpeted with odd-looking ferns that nobody was familiar with. Terry described them as looking like cleaning brushes. The terrain was very rugged and foreboding to the ladies wearing shorts.

Only Art was able to plow through the obstructing briers to a large rock that stood in the center of the gully. He clung to whatever was necessary to get down there. On his descent, Art identified and pointed out clumps of poisonous mushrooms. That was the first time we had seen anything poisonous all day. Even standing at the edge of the forest, it was dark and forbidding. I wondered how so many things could grow with so little sunlight reaching the forest floor. As I looked up at the canopy, I realized there was not a single leaf on any of the trees. That seemed extremely unusual for the middle of August, and I wondered if they were all dead.

Jim attempted to circle around through the forest to enter the gully from the other side. He finally made it and stood directly across the gully, facing the rest of us. The majority of us had only made it about fifteen feet into the woods, just past the initial onslaught of briers. Vicky, however, walked about ten feet further than the rest of us, where she clung to a tree overlooking the gully. Art walked around in a circle, sprinkling salt and reciting something out loud that Patricia later identified as the "K Cross."

According to Art's beliefs, this was done for our protection. I didn't put much merit in it. Such superstitions were contrary to my beliefs and something I chalked up to hocus-pocus. On the other hand, my sister was welcome to believe whatever she believed.

I recalled the words of the Apostle John when he said, "*Greater is He that is in you, than he that is in the world*" (1 John 4:4). My faith was in the Spirit of God and nothing else. If God Himself couldn't protect us from a fallen angel or an evil spirit, certainly a handful of salt would never be sufficient to get the job done. I couldn't help but think to myself that I would have been much more engaged if Art had sprinkled holy water on the ground. The circle of salt was approximately fifteen feet in diameter, and the rock Art stood on was directly in the center.

Art pointed to Vicky and asked if she felt anything. Her response was, "No." He then pointed to my sister and asked her if she felt anything. Her response was also "No." Lastly, he pointed to Jim. Everyone's response was, "No." Art then commented that "There is a definite blocking of psychic phenomena when three very good psychics feel nothing in a place like this."

He again pointed to Vicky and asked if she felt anything. Shivering and crying as she spoke, she held the tape recorder in one hand and my father's rock in the other. As she wrapped her arms around the tree that she had been clinging to, she recorded her response. By the time she finished, she was a wreck. She slumped around the base of the tree like a wet blanket that had been tossed there.

Vicky never stopped hugging the tree; she just slid down it as she talked, unaware that she was scratching and cutting her arms. Tears ran down her face, and her voice shook and cracked as she spoke. If she was acting, it was an Academy Award-winning performance. Everyone was drawn to her; the hair stood up on everyone's arms. We definitely were paying attention.

Vicky spoke in broken fragments rather than standard speech or conversation. She said we were intruding in a meeting place. There was a group of twenty-two people, both male and female, that met there. She saw the people, and they were short in stature. They were people who had influenced many world events in the past. Their influence had not been good. They were currently short their required number and had to fill their vacancies before they could again be active. As Vicky finished speaking, Art chimed in like he had been talking all along. "I don't think we have to worry about them finding the four people they need."

Art then pointed to my sister for a second time and asked if she felt anything. I could tell Patricia felt nervous and scared. My sister hesitated for a second and then answered, "I feel the cold, but anything else will have to wait for me to dream about tonight." She then nervously waved her hand to the left and kept talking, "Should we move a little bit more over in this direction? Are you sure we're in the right spot?" Patricia later confessed she was definitely blocking any potential psychic phenomena at that point. She saw what Vicky had just experienced, and she wanted nothing to do with it.

Art then turned and pointed to Jim. Before Art could speak, Jim said, "Nothing." Still facing Jim, Art raised both his arms in the air, both bent at the elbows, like a right-hand turn signal, but with both arms. He asked Jim to walk toward him through the circle of salt. Jim questioned Art about doing this and jokingly commented that the overgrowth was too thick. That was the first time I had heard Jim question Art in nearly two days. I can only guess he must have been apprehensive. After some insistence on Art's part, Jim did as he requested. Jim walked across the center of the circle and then repositioned himself outside of it again. He sat on the ground, facing Art, with his back toward the rest of us.

With his arms still in the air, Art turned to face my sister. Everyone knew he was going to ask her to walk toward him through the circle of salt. He tried, but Patricia wouldn't budge. He asked her several times, but she continued to refuse. As Patricia later recalled, she felt as though her feet were firmly planted on the ground. Conscious and hyper-aware of everything going on around her, my sister took several pictures and remembered in great detail each picture that she took and in what order.

Still looking at her, Art lowered his arms. Although Patricia was disappointed Art seemed to have changed his mind about her crossing the circle, she felt as though she couldn't have climbed down the hill any further anyway. Perhaps Art had sensed her fear or inability to climb down the hill.

Completely unnoticed to anyone, the dog had been going nuts ever since we first entered the woods. He ran around in a large circle that formed a ring around everyone in the forest and centered on the gully. He ran and ran and ran, barking the entire time. It surprised me I had not noticed his behavior earlier. Ozzie was a full-grown black lab, and he barked loudly. He ran around in circles so fast that at one point, his hind legs slid out from under him and became lodged between two good-sized rocks. Oblivious to his predicament, Ozzie scraped the rocks in front of him, frantically pulling himself forward until he was free. Then he was off and running again.

Patricia later told us she was worried the dog would break a leg and wondered why Dad hadn't yelled at him to settle down. I think nobody yelled at the dog because nobody had noticed the dog until then. Ozzie had been good all day; this was the first time he had acted up. My father turned to Ginger, pointed at the dog, and said, "This is the place."

As quickly as we noticed Ozzie's behavior, it came to an end. The dog stopped in front of Ginger and began digging a hole between two rocks at her feet. Although several of us saw the dog digging the hole, it never occurred to any of us to see what was buried there, if anything. I couldn't shake the feeling of being an observer to a play that was taking place in front of me. I felt as though no matter what I did, the outcome would be the same. Art and Vicky never noticed the dog. They were so engrossed in what they were seeing that they missed everything else.

Jim sitting down is the last thing that my sister or I remember happening in the gully. The dog stopped digging and everyone except Jim started to walk back up the hill toward the road where our vehicles were parked. I vaguely remember someone helping me walk Vicky back to the road. She appeared to be catatonic and never said a word, but nobody seemed concerned. Nobody said anything. We each grabbed an arm and helped Vicky to her feet. It was like we were all sleepwalking in a dream and never woke up until we got back to the side of the road.

When we reached the road, the conversation resumed like it had never stopped. Nobody mentioned why we had all walked out of the woods at the same time or why Vicky was catatonic two minutes ago, but was now fine. It just didn't seem odd to anyone at the time.

Art blurted out, "This was the most evil place I have ever been." I made a mental note that it was the first time all day Art had used the word "evil." He later told Patricia that although he had only heard the recollection a few weeks prior to the trip, he now felt like "it had been in his head for a thousand years. It was real."

Art suggested they give Jim a few minutes to meditate before they called him back up to the road. That's when Ann and I decided we needed to take a little break, to separate ourselves from the tension in the air. It had been a long day, and I am sure we all felt a little emotionally and physically drained. Ann and I walked along the other side of the road.

The trees on this side of the road appeared healthier and further apart. The floor of the forest was carpeted with the wild ferns that you would expect to see in this area of Pennsylvania. About fifteen feet into the woods, we found a clearing. There appeared to be an old access or logging road leading further into the woods. A fifteen-foot-wide strip of trees had been cleared out for something a long time ago. Now overgrown with field grass, it looked like an old road. Ann and I probably walked a hundred feet up the peaceful road before we turned around.

Although I didn't speak it at the time, Blair's Gap had not yet been resolved, at least not for me. I would need to come back by myself without the psychics like my father and I were meant to do almost a decade earlier. As we passed back through the clearing on our way back to the vehicles, I remember having the thought that, "This is where I should camp. This is where I should meet him." I didn't tell anyone, but I had already made up my mind that I would be coming back.

Then I heard a voice in my head that said, "I may have played with them, but I'll speak with you." As soon as I heard it, I attributed it to my imagination, but I had allowed the seed to be planted. The words played over and over again in my mind. Like my father, I permitted Blair's Gap to become an entity unto itself by choosing to ignore thoughts that were allowed to feed on one another, unchecked for the next thirty years.

When we made it back to the vehicles, Jim had already come out of the woods and was talking to everyone. Patricia asked him if he was able to see anything when he had been left by himself alone in the woods to meditate. Jim said he saw a few things. He described a stone wheel with thirteen spokes, a flying white bat that fell out of the sky, and a pond with ripples. The ripples were expanding outward from the center like a rock had been tossed in the middle of the pond.

Patricia then said, "Well, we accomplished what we set out to do. I suppose we'll see the total effect over the next few months." Jim then agreed that was probably what the ripples in the pond meant. I am certain neither one of them knew how right they were at the time.

My father said he had no doubt this was the right place. As I recall, he looked quite pale. Patricia asked him what he had seen to make him say that. In his typical, mysterious fashion, my father said, "You wouldn't believe me if I told you." Ever persistent, Patricia prodded our father to tell her what he had seen. Finally, Dad said, "I'll tell you later. I don't want to tell you in front of everyone else."

That turned out to be never. Months later, when Patricia followed up with our father, he denied seeing anything, but questioned her extensively about what she thought she had seen. That was my father—the master of avoidance. He would always turn a situation around to you.

On the drive back to the campsite, we passed a clearing in the forest with a stone monument that stood about a hundred feet off the road. Art pulled his car over to the side of the road and everybody followed him to the shoulder. Patricia then got out of Art's car to walk back and ask the others to back up to the monument. As she approached the second car, Jim stuck his head out of the driver's side window and yelled, "He wants us to back up to the monument to the trees." Before Patricia could answer, Jim began to back up. I followed suit, and we all backed up the road about fifty feet to the clearing in front of the monument.

Vicky still gripped my father's rock in her hands when she got out of the lead vehicle. Everyone had gathered at the monument when she noticed the green in my father's rock begin to glow. This time she pointed it out to both Patricia and Ginger who both claimed to have seen it.

I didn't see it, but one thing was for sure, it was getting dark and the sun was definitely not reflecting off the rock this time. Art asked everyone to gather around the monument for a group photo. As we gathered on either side of the monument, somebody read the dedication and sure enough, Jim was right. It was a monument to the trees. Patricia was convinced our group pictures would be some of the most important pictures of the day. She was positive that "something else" would show up in those particular pictures.

I was starting to feel more like myself and a little skeptical. It felt to me like we were back at Crystal Springs. It was as though they had turned something on, and now they couldn't turn it off. Those admittedly "blocking" at Blair's Gap were now on sensory overload. I'd had about all I could take for one day. The ride back to camp was a quiet and uneventful one. Patricia described Art as being preoccupied and noticed that Vicky finally set my father's rock down when we turned off Highway 666.

Back at camp, we ate our picnic lunch that was now supper. Everyone seemed exhausted and drained. Even the dog that would typically roam from person to person looking for leftovers ate sitting up rather than his usual practice of standing. Then Ozzie fell over on his side and lay there like he was too tired to even do that.

I hardly remember any conversation at camp. Patricia said later the lack of conversation was extremely peculiar, especially for Art. In the past, "psychic work" would always wind everyone up like a top, and talking about what they had experienced would be the way everyone would unwind and release their pent-up energy. Patricia said she would have expected the camp to be full of excitement, comparing notes and discussing the events of the day. Instead, everyone seemed lost in their own thoughts. Art and Vicky, who had planned to stay for the weekend, drove home that night. Ann and I did the same. We were tired and wanted to get home, to sleep in our own bed, to put the weekend behind us. We hardly spoke on the six-hour drive.

When the photographs taken that weekend were developed, only one photograph revealed something odd and unexpected. It was a photograph taken at Blair's Gap by my sister. In the photograph, a man seems to be floating four or five inches above the ground. Nobody recognized the man or his clothing, and my sister remembers taking the photograph with nobody in the frame.

What sets heaviest on my mind today are the pond and the ripples. My sister had no idea how right she was when she said, "I suppose we'll see the total effect over the next few months." When I got home, I put the weekend behind me and went on with my life.

Gradually, I heard a small voice. At first the voice was my own. I remembered my thoughts from Blair's Gap: "This is where I should camp. This is where I should meet him." Eventually, I heard the voice say, "I may have played with them, but I'll speak with you." Over time, the voice became louder and menacing.

It played over and over in my head like a broken record. My thoughts fed upon themselves and grew to nearly overcome me. Self-preservation kept me from wanting to acknowledge the voice, or worse yet, respond to it. I fought hard to suppress the voice and my thoughts. I convinced myself it was not a voice at all; it was only my imagination gone amok after witnessing Vicky's psychic encounter.

Later in my life, I heard the voice as clear as day. It was the traveler calling me, taunting me, saying, "I'll speak with you!" It was like a festering wound that refused to heal without the attention it demanded. My direction seemed predetermined and unavoidable. I needed to do something drastic. I needed to amputate and cauterize.

8

EVIL INCARNATE

Inheriting the Stone

It's funny how so many seemingly unrelated events intertwine to form the chapters of our lives. As they occur, we never recognize them for what they are or the impact they've had on our lives. Only years later do we see how the puzzle pieces came together to form the person we have become. How the puzzle turns out and the picture the puzzle creates, good or bad, tells the story of our character. Sometimes we need to stop and reflect on that picture, recognize it for what it is, and use it as a stepping stone to healing. It's not the things we went through or the things that happened to us, it is what we did about those things and how we handled them that others will remember and we will live with.

After thirty-plus years of marriage, it is easy to see how a man could go temporarily insane after losing his better half, or in the case of my father, his compass and grounding rod. At least, that's the excuse I tell myself when I look back at what happened to my father after my mother's passing.

My mother was my father's recovery nurse when he lost a half a lung during the Korean War; it was a true love story. Mother was the glue that held my father together, and it was her faith that kept his demons in check. Though somewhat restricted by her Catholic doctrine, my mother had a true love of Jesus Christ and His teachings. My father, on the other hand, had no such spiritual or religious affiliation and let my mother be his guide. She was his moral compass, and his faith was in her. My father loved my mother with all his heart, and he was lost without her—a broken man. After a while he dated some local ladies and some friends of friends, but never again could he kindle the flame he once shared with my mother.

Then one day to my surprise, my father announced he was bringing over someone he wanted me to meet, a woman he had been dating and was getting serious about. After meeting her, my father asked me what I thought of her. I made a joke about her having a gap between her two front teeth that was large enough to toss a nickel through from across the room without touching her gums. We both laughed, and I told him it didn't much matter what I thought as long as he was happy. I went on to say that I would be happy if he married a two-headed goat as long as it made him happy. That was a big mistake and something I would later regret saying.

Within six months, my father had married the woman he had introduced me to. As we later learned, she was an ex-inmate from the prison where my father worked and was out on a work-release program when I met her. Her story was that she had been incarcerated for extortion. I learned from a fellow prison guard that she was actually in prison for manslaughter, or as I call it, the murder of her husband.

Sometime between buying the shell of a cabin on the Pennsylvania border for a penny and a song and putting his house up for sale in Medina, my father retired and started dating the woman from Albion Correctional. By the time he had completed construction of the inside of the cabin, he had married the woman I came to believe was evil incarnate. My father entered the relationship naively, trusting his new wife to be the moral compass my mother was. What he found though was much different. His new wife was self-centered, cold, and manipulative. She eventually crushed his spirit.

Some explanation is required here, lest the reader think I haven't forgiven my father's second wife for the wickedness she inflicted on our family. I absolutely have forgiven her. "*Vengeance is mine sayeth the Lord,*" Scripture says, and I will let Him have it. I will not go through my life harboring hatred.

But there is value in telling her story because it brought my father's journey to an end and strengthened me to alter the course of my own journey. I will not accept destiny or a predetermined end; my end shall be of my own accord. This woman was truly evil and may still be alive by sheer meanness and spite.

Regardless of whatever truth I may share in the telling of her story, if she is still alive, I fear reprisal. It is for that reason I will call my father's second wife Belle, a pseudonym in remembrance of the evil Belle Gunness, a Norwegian-American serial killer who killed many of her suitors and boyfriends, as well as two of her own daughters.

Belle projected an evil that would linger, an evil that would pop up and rear its ugly head when it was least expected. Her power was in being able to put her prey at ease while she baited her trap, implemented her plan, and sharpened her knife in anticipation of the kill. She was very good at dropping a word here and there that left enough doubt to cause one to ever so slightly change the way they were thinking about something without realizing it. That was the power she used to distance my father from my sister and me. It was insidious, sliding into place without notice. She could talk you into climbing into the trunk of her car without knowing you were in the trunk until the trunk lid closed and the lights went out.

I was in my early twenties at the time my father died and never put all the pieces together until much later. Now that I am in my late fifties and still working out of necessity, I realize that my father was barely fifty when all this happened to him. He was only sixty-two when he died, not that much older than I am now. I assumed my dad had a retirement from the state, and I knew that after a while he started collecting his Social Security, but there were signs. He was a proud man and never said anything, but I wish he had. I was in a position to help him out financially at the time. My sister and I surmised after his death that early retirement must have meant being forced to leave after twenty-five years of service with no pension due to his association with Belle.

I helped my father write a resume, and he later went to work for the Allegany Sheriff's Department. He worked part-time and as much as he could without impacting his Social Security. Belle on the other hand still excelled at the fine art of deception. She lied on her application and got a nice federal job at the Little Genesee Post Office for several years until they discovered she was an ex-felon. When she lost her job, word got out about her time in prison and she wasn't able to contribute much financially after that.

I attempted to get along with Belle at first, but as time went on, the indicators of my father's discontent were apparent. I didn't notice them at first and attributed her odd behavior and my negative thoughts to imagination. I just figured Belle was not my mother, and I couldn't possibly expect either my father or myself to have the same relationship with her that we had with my mother for so many years. After all, I only saw Belle three or four times a year for a few days at time when I drove down to visit with my father or he drove up to visit with me.

My sister saw it for what it was much sooner than I did. The signs were always much clearer for her. Whenever she called my father, or for that matter, whenever I called my father, Belle would always answer the phone. Belle would then tell my sister that my father was sleeping, not at home, or working outside and that she would have him call her back when he returned or got up, but he never did. My father generally called to talk with my sister when Belle was away buying groceries and typically ended the call when she returned.

For my sister, Belle once planted a seed that took nearly ten years to fully bloom. Patricia had inherited a pearl necklace from our mother that was originally given to her as a gift by her mother-in-law, our grandmother. Nora was still alive after my mother's passing and told Patricia that she had originally given the pearls to our mother because she figured anyone else in the family would have sold them by then. The pearls were from the Sir Francis Drake estate and worth considerable money. Attempting to get them appraised for her insurance, Patricia took the pearls to a reputable jeweler. The jeweler confirmed they were real pearls of the right age and from the correct location, but told her she would have to take them to a specialist for a true appraisal.

My sister treasured her pearls and kept them in a safe place. Years later, after my father's passing and while my sister was helping to dress her daughter for her first communion, she went to retrieve her pearls and found them to be pink in color and peeling. Then she remembered, but it was too late to do anything about it. Patricia had once lent the pearls to Belle shortly after she married our father. Belle said she knew a reputable jeweler who would fix the broken clasp and restring the pearls for her for virtually nothing. My father had truly brought a viper into the family. None of us could fathom the extent of damage that she could inflict.

I am not sure if Belle was jealous of my sister's relationship with my father, or just outright didn't like her, but one thing was for sure, she tried everything in her power to distance the relationship between them. I, on the other hand, paid my penance; if I endured a mandatory fifteen minutes of conversation with Belle, she would eventually allow me to speak with my father on the phone. Unfortunately, by that time, I had already told Belle what I had intended to tell my father. I had to repeat myself; it was like she had taken the wind out of my sails.

Belle liked to stir up hate and discontent. She worked endlessly to separate family members through rumor and innuendo. Whenever the opportunity presented itself, Belle said or implied terrible things about my sister and her husband and the raising of their two daughters, things that I never entertained or would consider repeating. Years later, when my sister and I were able to compare notes, I discovered that on the few occasions when Belle was forced to speak with my sister, she had equally terrible things to say about me and my wife. I once asked my father when we were alone if he believed the things Belle had been saying about my sister's husband and her children. He said he absolutely did not and that if he did, he would be on his way down to get his grandbabies. I wondered at the time why he never corrected Belle, but now that I am older, I understand the evil that he lived with and feared.

A few years before my mother's passing and the release of Belle from Albion, my father was diagnosed with hepatitis C and was told to stop drinking. My father knew he had contracted hepatitis in Attica, but he never knew if he caught it from an inmate throwing feces at him or from another inmate who had bit him. Once diagnosed, my father stopped stocking the refrigerator with beer and drinking nearly every day as he did when I was growing up. Every now and then though, the temptation would overtake him, and he would have to slip away for a few beers. He missed the social interaction and camaraderie that he felt with his friends at the bar. Twice after I moved back east, once while my mother was alive and once after her passing, I had to go get my father at the bar because he was too drunk to drive home.

After marrying Belle, I was not at all surprised when my father asked me to ride along with him while he went to get his paycheck from the Allegany Sheriff's Department. He cashed his check in a bar, hid a hundred-dollar bill in a fold of his wallet, and asked me not to tell Belle about it. From there we went to a party with my father's coworkers at the Allegany Sheriff's Department, narcotics division, and undercover agents. I drank a couple of beers, developed a headache, and ended up sleeping on the seat of my father's truck for an hour or so while he drank and talked with his coworkers. Eventually, my father had enough to drink, came and got me, and we drove back to the cabin.

Within five years, my father contracted cirrhosis of the liver on top of his hepatitis C, and his health went downhill rather rapidly from there. Shortly after my father's diagnosis, he phoned to ask me if I would be willing to sign a document giving me authority to execute his living will. Belle was on the phone with him when he called, and I, of course, agreed immediately. He had his lawyer draw up the papers and mailed them to me within a couple of days for my signature. I immediately signed them, made copies, and return mailed them to my father. As life turned out, I was not able to grant my father his last request—to be buried next to my mother in Guitonville, Pennsylvania. As a matter of fact, I was only able to see my father twice more before he died.

At first, my father's spirits were upbeat. My dad told me he had always wanted to learn to play the guitar, so I gave him one of my old guitars with a book of easy chord changes to some old Bob Dylan songs and we played with that for a couple of days. At that point, Dad wasn't able to work any longer and asked to borrow some money I brought along with me.

The next and the last time I saw my father alive, he was in much worse shape. His already large stomach was now bloated and full of fluids that his liver could no longer process. It had become very difficult and uncomfortable for my dad to drive. He asked me to drive him to the hospital in Sayre, Pennsylvania, where they would drain the fluid off his abdomen and perform some additional tests. We talked a lot on the drive, and when we got back, my father twice asked me to sort through his tools and take what I wanted. I refused as it seemed to do so would be to acknowledge he was dying.

As we walked back to the cabin from the barn, I told my father I wished it had been one of his kidneys so I could give him one of mine. My father told me they could do a transplant with just a piece of a liver and the rest of it would grow back in time. My response was something stupid like, "I didn't know that," but I made up my mind in that moment to give him a piece of my liver. I just needed four or five days to get my head wrapped around the idea. Unfortunately, I drove home that night and never said a word to my father about my intentions, and he died two days later. It is the biggest regret of my life. If I had just said something before I left, he may have hung on long enough to get his transplant.

When I was notified of my dad's passing, I left work, picked up my wife, and immediately drove down to the cabin. Virtually, that same evening, Belle's zebra stripes were revealed. When I arrived at the cabin, Belle's four children from a previous marriage had already arrived and I was informed there would be no room in the inn for my sister and family who were on their way up from Whitehall, Pennsylvania. That seemed unusually cruel to me that my sister could not visit my father's house or be around our relatives. After all, she was his only daughter and his favorite. It was the middle of the winter in a town of less than a hundred people. Luckily, I arranged through one of my cousins to have a room opened up at a local lodge that had already closed down for the winter.

Things weren't much better at church the next day. It was a memorial service with no body since my father had always wanted to be cremated. Belle had preassigned seats with my sister and her family seated together by themselves on the other side of the church. Ann and I ignored our assigned seats with Belle and went over to sit with my sister, her husband, and their two girls. That upset Belle to no end, and she made it known to all who would listen. Belle was never one to exercise much restraint unless it was to her advantage. Her mouth generally had direct access to her thoughts.

While I was leaving the memorial service, I really began to feel the loss of my father. Each side of the entire front sidewalk was lined with prison guards from Attica and Albion Correctional. They wore their dress uniforms with black tape over their badges and raised their swords for Belle, my sister, and me to walk under. I burst into tears when they raised their swords, and my sister helped me to my car. Our families exited the church after us, and we all went from there to a wake that was being held at a local bar in one of the neighboring towns.

My father had many friends and coworkers who had driven down for the memorial service, so the wake was crowded. As

I recall, my sister, her husband, and their girls stayed for the entire gathering. Belle, on the other hand, sat at a table for an hour or so with her daughters. Knowing full well that everyone handles death a little differently, I didn't give it another thought when I noticed Belle was distant and unsociable. After all, her husband had just died and she didn't know a lot of my father's friends. It must have been quite uncomfortable for her. Looking back on it now, I see her more as a self-appointed matriarch waiting for her minions to come over and address her.

Like my sister, I knew almost everyone at the wake. They were either relatives or prison guards I had seen off and on with my parents since childhood. It was customary for prison guards to tie one on in honor of the deceased when one of their own had died and that was exactly what they were doing. I made the rounds, played some pool, had several drinks, and was pretty drunk as I recall by the time my wife half carried me out the back door wearing a prison guard's hat.

Ann drove me back to the cabin. Between taking Belle to the funeral home, helping to select an urn, choosing pictures for the memorial service, plowing the driveway, and stocking up on firewood, I had been up for a couple of days at that point and decided to take a nap on the floor. Ann and I had thrown some covers and pillows down the night before to fashion a bed in the corner of the front room. While I was sleeping, somebody mentioned something about giving the eldest son the funeral flag. Not recognizing or acknowledging the sentimental value of the flag, Belle said she would contact the VFW to see if she could get a duplicate flag. I slept for probably two hours. When I got up, Ann informed me Belle's sons, Kenny and Tim, had been out in the barn for the last two hours, loading up Kenny's truck with my father's tools.

I remembered my father had offered me his tools two weeks earlier, but I had refused to take them as I didn't want to admit he was dying. I bit my lip and told Belle I would like to pass my father's oxy-acetylene tanks down to my son, Mike. I told her the tanks now required a special license to acquire, but that if you already had them, you fell under a grandfather clause that would allow you to keep them. Belle said she would have Kenny and Tim set them aside for me. I had driven the car down, so I told Belle I would return in a couple of weeks with my truck to pick them up.

Ann and I stayed another day or so, but I had to get back to work and was forced to leave before my father's ashes were back from the crematorium. We left with the understanding that Belle would keep the ashes at the cabin until everyone who was interested was available to go down to Guitonville together where we would then bury the ashes next to my mother.

Before I left, Belle told me the duplicate flag was in her bedroom, on top of her dresser. When I went to her room to retrieve the flag, the two flags were stacked one on top of the other. There was no way to know which of the flags was used for the memorial service. That's when I knew. To Belle, these were not mementos of someone you loved and lost, they were only things.

After I got home, I thought about Belle shutting my sister out and giving my father's tools away before he was even in the ground. I thought about how disrespectful of my father she had been, and I stewed on it for two days. I called her on Wednesday and announced that Mike and I would be coming down on Saturday morning with my truck to pick up Dad's oxy-acetylene tanks. Belle told me Kenny and Tim had set them aside for me and that they were locked up in her basement.

On Thursday, Belle called to tell me her heart had been racing and she had checked herself into the hospital in Olean. I think she hoped I would change my plans. I didn't. Still in the hospital, Belle called me again on Friday to ask if I would stop by Fulton and pick up her sister and give her a ride down to the cabin. I had a small truck with a single bench seat and a standard shift, but I agreed.

When we arrived at the cabin, Belle's sister said she had to freshen up, went immediately into Belle's bedroom, and then shut the door. I assumed she was hiding my father's ashes or whatever else Belle had put her up to. I quickly scanned the room and realized the place had been stripped bare. There was not a single picture, knickknack, or anything personal that belonged to my father anywhere in sight.

Mike and I went out to my truck to get our overnight bags. When I returned, I saw the Blair's Gap stone sitting on the hearth next to the woodstove. It looked very much out of place. With everything else now absent from the cabin, I pictured someone packing boxes on the floor, recognizing the stone had no monetary value, and setting it aside to be forgotten.

What happened next is hard to describe. In just a fraction of a second, my stomach tightened and all the memories of the recollection, my mother's table, the stone, and the man in the mirror came flooding back. It was like walking into a closed door; it stopped me dead in my tracks. It had been a long time since I had entertained any such thoughts. I had done a good job of suppressing them all, pretending like those things had never happened. But there it was, staring me right in the face again.

I don't know if it was the sudden loss of my father, the evil that my father had endured at the hands of the woman I now call Belle, or the not-so-faint memory of the man in the mirror, but of one thing I was certain, this was not just a bunch of childhood memories I preferred to forget. This was unfinished business that needed to be addressed. My father's appointment was now my appointment. I needed to discover the secret of the stone. I scooped it up in the palm of my hand just as Belle's sister opened the bedroom door. I then made my way back to my truck where I quickly put the stone in my glove compartment before heading back inside.

Mike and I both took our bags up to the loft where we had planned to sleep that night. I opened the attic door and my worst thoughts were confirmed. The attic had also been stripped clean. All that remained were several empty packing boxes and three or four framed pictures of my grandmother that appeared to have been thrown in there. It had been less than two weeks since my father's passing. Mike and I went back downstairs and asked Belle's sister if she was ready for us to take her over to the hospital in Olean to see her sister. She said she was so we headed out.

I don't remember if it was from talking to someone at the hospital or from reading her chart, but at the hospital I learned that Belle had suffered a panic attack. At that point, I was just doing what I needed to do to get through it all. I tried to be cordial and told Belle I would like to have my father's badges from Attica, Albion, and the Sheriff's Department as mementos, and my sister would like to have some of the old family photographs. We all visited with Belle for about an hour before Mike and I excused ourselves so that I could go smoke a cigarette. When we returned, Belle said my cousin had a set of keys to the cabin and had come over and unlocked the basement door so Mike and I could load up the oxy-acetylene tanks when we returned. That seemed odd, but I didn't question it.

It was already late in the afternoon when Mike and I returned to Belle's room. We left shortly thereafter with Belle's sister. As I recall, we all stopped to get some fast food from Arby's and headed back to the cabin. Once we got there, Belle's sister went into the cabin while Mike and I walked around to the basement entrance where we found the basement to be much like the rest of the cabin. Except for the furnace, breaker boxes, and Mike's tanks, the basement was completely bare. We loaded up the tanks, went upstairs, and talked with Belle's sister until she was ready to go to bed. Mike and I then also called it a night and headed back up to the loft. It was hot in the loft as it always was, and neither one of us got much sleep. Mike and I got up early, said our good-byes to Belle's sister, and headed back home.

About a week later, Belle called to ask me about my father's shotgun. She told me she had been looking all over for it. She couldn't find it and thought that someone must have broken into the cabin while she was in the hospital and stolen it. I should have kept my mouth shut, but it felt good telling her that I took it because it had sentimental value to me. Knowing I would never see the money she owed me, I even offered to call it even for the $1,500 she had borrowed from me, but Belle was having nothing to do with it. It appeared I had given her the out she had been looking for. A few days later, I received a restraining order from Belle's attorney. It forbade me from being anywhere in the vicinity of the cabin.

A few weeks later, I received another phone call from Belle to tell me my father's ashes had come back from the crematorium, but she had accidently spilled them. It was not only bizarre, but extremely disrespectful of my father, so I asked her how that happened. She told me she had tried opening up the ashes to look at them and accidently spilled them. I asked her why she tried to open up the urn, and she said she was curious, and then asked, "Who wouldn't be?" My first thoughts were that only an amoral, psychopathic, murdering ex-con with no concept of right or wrong would be curious, but I kept my mouth shut. I had two dogs that had been cremated and never had the urge to look at their ashes.

My aunt Donna believed with all her heart and was very vocal in proclaiming that Belle had poisoned my father and that my evil stepmother sifted through my father's ashes, looking for bone fragments or teeth that could be tested and used as evidence to prosecute her. I thought that was far-fetched. Instead, I assumed she was just trying to inflict more pain on us.

I then reminded Belle about my father's last wish to be buried next to my mother. She said that my father had always enjoyed the Adirondacks and that she might bury him there. Belle never asked me about the Blair's Gap stone. She had completely forgotten about setting it on the hearthstone; it meant nothing to her. One thing was for sure, my father never told Belle about the recollection or the stone. For some selfish reason, it was comforting to know that my father had kept at least a few secrets from Belle.

Belle continued to spew her venom well after my father's death. Using her own perverse logic and my father's friendship as bait, Belle lured one of my father's dearest friends into a snare that was fully beyond my ability to even imagine. There was never any question after that as to where Belle drew the line. She didn't. Everything was justifiable; nothing was sacred, and no lie was too great. Several weeks after my father had died and just a few weeks after Belle stopped talking to me, I received a call from Aunt Donna. She told me in confidence that she had heard from one of my father's dearest friends who was now in trouble.

Belle had convinced this friend to come to the cabin to talk with her about something she couldn't discuss over the phone. When he got there, she asked him if she could borrow $10,000. When my father's friend told Belle he didn't have $10,000 to lend her, she fixed him a drink. He took a few sips, and the next thing he remembered was waking up naked in her bed. Belle told him he might want to reconsider lending her the $10,000 now that he had spent the night with her—in her bed—and she had pictures to prove it.

I told Donna my father's friend needed to nip this in the bud, or the $10,000 would only be the start of her blackmail. Without delay, he needed to tell his wife exactly what happened so that Belle would have nothing to hold over his head. Donna passed my advice along to my father's friend, and I think he must have taken it as he appeared to live out the remainder of his life in peace.

Needless to say, our family was never able to bury my father's ashes next to my mother, I never received the badges I had asked for, and my sister never got the family pictures she requested.

Within three months, Belle had a new live-in boyfriend, and within six months, the cabin was auctioned off for back taxes. Belle and her new boyfriend eventually moved back to Schroon Lake, where she came from. Assuming her boyfriend is still alive, I wish him well. The devil incarnate—Belle—had made the end of my father's life a living hell.

As for me, I walked away with a well-used set of oxy-acetylene tanks, an imaginary $1,500 shotgun, the Blair's Gap stone, and an appointment with the traveler in the woods. It was high time I took down the sails, taking the wind out of this recurring nightmare known as Blair's Gap, and set my own course in life. For only having met the traveler once and never having uttered a single word to him, I knew now he had controlled far too much of my life and ruined my father's life. It was time to put an end to him.

Remembering how my great-grandfather, a preacher, had begun to follow the traveler into the woods, I questioned my own character and the strength of my faith. Would I succumb to evil? Would I trade my eternal soul for a momentary pleasure? I secretly hoped it was nothing more than my imagination, a confused memory blown out of proportion, something I built up in my mind over the years, and that there would be nothing waiting for me at Blair's Gap except a cold and lonely night spent alone in the woods.

If it was anything more than that, I surely needed to prepare myself for the encounter. I needed to dry my powder and sharpen my axe. If I was ever going to find true peace in this life and avoid the hell that was my father's life, I needed to take a leap of faith. To be free of my father's burden and this curse, I needed to blindly step off that forbidding cliff into the darkness and unknown. It would start by researching the stone and immersing myself in God's Word.

9

FATHER'S TABLE

Armor of God

If I learned anything from my multi-year introspective and vision quest, it was that many of my beliefs had little basis and I still had as many questions as I had answers. Digesting those facts, I realized that I didn't know much of anything that I could refer to as truth.

I was about twenty-five when I set out in life to find the truth of God and Christ. It started around the time of my divorce and shortly after moving back east to go to college. I was helping my mother go through some boxes in her basement when I came across a small box of books. Near the top was the King James Bible that Nora had bought me for my twelfth birthday. The front cover had been folded over and held there for years by another book. When I folded the flap back over, I saw where my name had been embossed in red ink. I remembered how much I loved that Bible when I was an altar boy. It made me sad to see that it wound up there in a box of old books in my mother's basement. I took it out of the box, dusted it off, and kept it.

I thought about many things over the next few days. I thought about how my ex-wife's love of reading had taught me to appreciate reading for entertainment and fun. I thought about all the books I didn't care about, but would have to read before I finished college. I wondered how I would explain to God how I had found the time to read so many books, but never found the time to read His.

So, I committed to reading that Bible from cover to cover, just a little bit each night, sometimes just until I could turn a page, just as Nora did for her entire life. The more I read it, the more I became aware that many organized religions based their beliefs on only a portion of the Bible or added something that wasn't there.

In searching out my faith, I found myself most comfortable in non-denominational, Christ-based churches. They seemed to be the only churches that recognized the coming and dwelling of the Holy Spirit, the differences between the Old Testament and the New Testament, the law that defeats us, and the laws that save us. By my second or third time through, I was beginning to truly understand God's love and what He had done for me. I was establishing a relationship with the Lord, and I was beginning to hear the voice of the Holy Spirit.

As I put Christ into perspective, I found guidance and understanding for many other aspects of my life. I was fourteen when I first saw the traveler and nearly thirty at the time of the reminder. By the time I reached the age of thirty, I was aware that thoughts of Blair's Gap and the old man would haunt me for the entirety of my life if I let them. They were memories that needed to be addressed, unexplained events that required clarification, and nightmares that needed to be put to bed. It was a confrontation I would not take lightly, a final conflict that would require preparation.

Sometime after the reminder, during the peak of my working career, while my wife and I stumbled through raising our two boys, I drifted away from what is important in life and found myself wrapped up in the material aspects of survival. It started by working at a nuclear power plant during construction, twelve hours a day, seven days a week for two years. It was easy to justify not having time to go to church or read the Bible and just as easy to say I needed a bigger house or my wife deserved better. Suddenly, I had a problem with my temper and patience. It took me so many years to recognize my failures. Only by the grace of God and the fellowship of Christians that God placed in my path, did I eventually find my way back home. I again began to pray with vigor.

After twenty-two years of working toward retirement, I found myself nine months short of a rollover to retirement, out of a job, and looking for a new career. In time, I realized that my loss was actually an answer to prayer. I survived for about two years before I was down to around $800 with no way to make the next mortgage payment. My wife was a trooper, but I could see she was seriously feeling the weight. I lifted up a desperate prayer to my Lord for help, and ten minutes later, I landed what turned out to be the highest-paying and best job of my life. I became a contracted consultant working at the various nuclear power plants throughout the United States.

At my first assignment in Wisconsin, I missed my wife and wondered if our marriage would survive the necessary long separations. I prayed for my family and sought comfort in the Bible. One night the Holy Spirit spoke to me in an audible voice and said, "This is your time on the mountain. Use it wisely."

Over the next five years and as many assignments, I wrote a book of Christian poetry, *First Vespers—Spiritual Verses of Hope and Inspiration*. My pastor would later refer to this book as the most inspirational book of devotion he had ever read, a book that took the King James Bible and made it understandable to the common man. I am thankful for all the lives that God will and has allowed me to touch with His words.

Sometime after *First Vespers* was published, and more significantly after the research I conducted to write *First Vespers* was complete, I recognized that preparation for an encounter with the traveler had similarities to preparing for a Passover dinner with Christ the King. It was not something to take lightly or be unprepared for. Scripture makes it clear that many are invited to the table, but few are prepared to take advantage of the opportunity. Jesus assures the believer they will have a moment with Him. I could no longer get by with my cordial thank yous and convenient memory loss or last-minute excuses and just not going. Whether with the traveler or the Lord, a moment with either might determine where I would spend eternity.

Meeting with either, one thing was for certain—my host would always know more about me than I would ever know about my host. I had dirty laundry scattered around for everyone to see. It was time to find a new suit, trim my beard, and clean up my act. I needed to do some serious studying, tie up some loose ends, and put some issues to bed. I needed to balance the books and be prepared for my inevitable few minutes.

It occurred to me that I already had the instructions necessary to prepare for a moment with the Lord, and if I was prepared for a moment with my Lord, I was certainly ready for whatever the traveler had to say. Greater is He that is in you, than he that is in the world. I proceeded on the assumption that I would have only one opportunity to get it right.

I knew full well that ". . . *we wrestle not against flesh and blood, but against principalities, against powers, against the rulers of the darkness of the world, against spiritual wickedness in high places*" (Ephesians 6:12).

I determined to honor my host by donning the full armor of God. I would stand against evil having my loins ". . . *girt about with truth,*" and wearing "*the breastplate of righteousness.*"

My feet would be shod ". . . *with the preparation of the gospel of peace*," and I would take ". . . *the shield of faith*" wherewith I would be able to ". . . *quench all the fiery darts of the wicked*," and I would ". . . *take the helmet of salvation, and the sword of the Spirit, which is the word of God: Praying always with all prayer and supplication in the Spirit*" (Ephesians 6:14–18).

I would start by sharpening the sword of the Spirit, which is the Word of God. I committed to read the Bible from cover to cover and then start over at the beginning again until it was part of me—until I knew what it was to live in the Word. I learned that the sword of the Spirit could always be sharper, and I will be sharpening it until the day I die as did my grandmother Nora. As my understanding of the truth of my salvation grew, so did my understanding of God's grace and my unworthiness.

In the Epistle of Paul to the Romans, Paul tells us "*That if thou shalt confess with thy mouth the Lord Jesus, and shalt believe in thine heart that God hath raised him from the dead, thou shalt be saved. For with the heart man believeth unto righteousness; and with the mouth confession is made unto salvation*" (Romans 10:9–10).

Armed with this knowledge, I knew God loved us first. God is not the purveyor of guilt. He doesn't hold the threat of hellfire over our heads. The Word says, "*The Lord is . . . longsuffering toward us, not willing that any should perish, but that all should come to repentance*" (2 Peter 3:9).

So, I took the leap of faith. I bowed before my Lord and wept as a child. I kissed His feet, and my Lord grabbed me under my armpits, stood me back on my feet, and placed His helmet of salvation upon my head. After wearing my Lord's helmet of salvation for a while and becoming comfortable with the feel of it on my head, I became aware that the remainder of God's armor would not be so easy to acquire.

My breastplate of righteousness came at a great cost. The breastplate required that I make every effort to walk in the path our Lord had laid out for us. This meant putting God first in my life—ahead of my wife, my children, and me. It meant involving God in every decision I made and living each day to bring Him glory. At first I labored with every decision and continually prayed I would not weaken to justify my own desires over His. I tested every word of the Spirit; if it was of God, it was without sin.

As I grew in my understanding, it became easier to know what pleased God. Even the mention of God in my life initially brought about accusations of self-righteousness. I worked hard not to be offended when people close to me said such things. Friends and family kept alive the sins of my past and held me accountable for what Christ had already forgiven me for. Though my old life was now dead, they struggled to keep it alive. Many waited to witness my daily imperfections so they might pounce and say, "See, you are no better than me. You are not worthy to call yourself His." I was no better than they, but I was worthy to be called His, as were they by the grace of God. Even I questioned why God would place His desire, His heart, and His Spirit in such a dirty and disheveled temple as this, but He did.

The Apostle Paul tells us in his letter to Timothy that when our time on earth is complete, "*Henceforth there is laid up for me a crown of righteousness, which the Lord, the righteous judge, shall give me at that day: and not to me only, but unto all them also that love his appearing*" (2 Timothy 4:8).

Just as each of us who are saved become a stone in the crown of Christ (Zechariah 9:16) so the secret acts of kindness and charity that we perform become heavenly jewels of righteousness. They are our offerings—our alms.

In the words of Jesus, "*Take heed that ye do not your alms before men, to be seen of them; otherwise ye have no reward of your*

Father which is in heaven. Therefore when thou doest thine alms, do not sound a trumpet before thee, as the hypocrites do in the synagogues and in the streets, that they may have glory of men. Verily I say unto you, they have their reward. But when thou doest alms, let not thy left hand know what thy right hand doeth: That thine alms may be in secret: and thy Father, which seeth in secret, himself shall reward you openly" (Matthew 6:1–4).

The older we get, the more rapidly the years slip away and the more apparent our mortality becomes. Our ability to glorify God and to store up riches in heaven is limited by our time here on earth, which is infinitely short next to eternity.

The Apostle Paul tells us in his letter to the Corinthians, "*Every man's work shall be made manifest: for the day shall declare it, because it shall be revealed by fire; and the fire shall try every man's work of what sort it is. If any man's work abides which he has built thereupon, he shall receive a reward. If any man's work shall be burned, he shall suffer loss; but he himself shall be saved; yet so as by fire*" (1 Corinthians 3:13–15).

If my crown of righteousness is to be forged from my breastplate of righteousness, surely the weight of my crown is dependent on the strength of my breastplate. Not unlike my sword of the Spirit that requires constant sharpening, my breastplate of righteousness will require constant strengthening and be a lifelong ambition.

I sought to gird my loins with truth. My search started by seeking the truth of God and my relationship with Him. As I sharpened my sword of the Spirit, I read the book of John and learned that God has only promised to answer righteous prayers. John put it this way: ". . . *this is the confidence that we have in him, that, if we ask anything according to his will, he heareth us: And if we know that he hears us, whatsoever we ask, we know that we have the petitions that we desired of him*" (1 John 5:14–15).

John also makes it clear that we must be a believer, be saved, and be a worshipper to know with confidence that our righteous prayers will be answered. He tells us, ". . . *we know that God heareth not sinners: but if a man be a worshipper of God, and doeth his will, him he heareth*" (John 9:31).

If we are in God and the Spirit of God is in us, it is easy to discern a worldly prayer from a righteous prayer of Godly intent. That said, I understood what King David meant when he said, "*Delight thyself in the* Lord: *and he shall give thee the desires of thine heart*" (Psalm 37:4). I am not saying that God does not answer worldly prayers, only that He has not promised to do so. God is God and God may do as He pleases. Certainly, God has answered worldly prayers for me before, sometimes not as I expected, and sometimes to my own detriment.

Following this enlightenment, I have had many opportunities to exercise a righteous prayer; however, one particular prayer comes to the forefront as a righteous prayer with Godly intent. It was a prayer I prayed many times for my beloved Aunt Dona. Although Dona had the tough exterior of a farmer's wife, she was in many ways a saintly woman who was loved by many. Dona was a selfless caregiver for most of her adult life and always put the needs of others before her own.

Dona's mother-in-law, May, never liked her, but Dona cared for her for many years. She fed her, bathed her, and emptied her bedpan. Dona never openly said a harsh word about May, even when the older woman lost her civility, began throwing feces, and called her terrible names. Years after May's passing, Dona began caring for her mother, Nora, who was by then nearly ninety. My father by then was a widower and moved nearer to his sister to help with the care of his mother. My grandmother lived another six years as I recall and remained active until just a few weeks before her passing.

I stopped in to visit her when she could no longer get out of bed and her only regret was that her eyes would no longer cooperate when it came to reading her Bible. One day Dona came in to fluff her mom's pillow and my grandmother told her she felt warm. Dona went next door to the bathroom to dampen a washcloth for Grandma's forehead, and when she returned a moment later, her mother was dead.

Several years prior to that, Dona's husband—my uncle Bill—had lost the fingers of his right hand in a corn-combining accident. Being a severe diabetic and an admitted alcoholic, Bill's recovery was difficult, but still he managed to run the farm and shoot a deer that year with his big toe, which had been fashioned into his right thumb. By the time my grandmother died, Bill had full-blown Lyme disease, a disease barely heard of then and seldom diagnosed. After living with Lyme disease for many years, Bill suffered extensive and irreversible nerve damage when finally diagnosed. Uncle Bill eventually required full care, which Dona provided as she gradually retired the farm.

It seemed only a short time after Bill's passing that Dona was diagnosed with lung cancer. Perhaps ten years earlier my mother had died from lung cancer. She underwent radical chemotherapy and radiation treatment. Her hair fell out, and in the last few weeks of her life, she suffered greatly. My mother died just eight months after her diagnosis on July 4, 1981, at the age of 51.

Dona elected not to undergo such radical treatment; rather, she chose to stay at home under the care of hospice, enjoy the time she had remaining, and take the medications her doctor prescribed for her. Dona lasted several months and seemed comfortable most of the time. I took two weeks of vacation from work and went to stay with my favorite aunt for one last visit. By then, Dona used a portable oxygen bottle she took with her everywhere she went. We talked a lot, drove down many roads she hadn't been down in a long time, and visited with some friends she hadn't seen in years. She was a beautiful woman.

During my visit, Dona often listened to tapes of Roy Orbison. She said she was so very lonely and hadn't anyone to take care of any longer. Roy Orbison reminded her of her late husband Bill, who she couldn't wait to see again. It was sad to hear her say such things because I knew that in her heart she had given up, but I also knew my sadness was selfish and based upon my own loss and not her happiness. I thought about Dona's giving nature and the selfless life of servitude she had lived. I thought about the peaceful and quick passing of my grandmother and the suffering of my mother for the last few weeks of her life.

My righteous prayer of Godly intent was, "Merciful God who art with me always, remember now the charity and kind heart of my aunt Dona who cared for so many at the expense of her own health. Remember I cry those who she cared for and those who she put before herself. My dear Lord, I pray, let her not suffer for she labored to relieve the suffering of so many. Dear God, care for her now and take her quickly. In Jesus' name I pray, Amen."

Dona passed away within a few short weeks after my visit. As many of us over fifty who drink coffee and never heard of a Keurig one-cup coffee machine do, she had a habit of warming up the coffee left in the pot from the night before while brewing a new pot. Coffee drinkers don't like to wait for their first cup in the morning. When Dona passed away, she was found sitting with her arms folded at the kitchen table. The buzzer was going off with her first cup of coffee still in the microwave. She had died in the one minute it took to warm up her first cup of coffee.

Some will view this answer to prayer as coincidence, but those who have seen a hundred prayers like this answered may not. Those skeptics will fulfill the prophesy, "*That seeing they may see, and not perceive; and hearing they may hear, and not understand; lest at any time they should be converted, and their sins should be forgiven them*" (Mark 4:12).

I pray continually for understanding and the strengthening of my faith. God broke me and corrected me many times. He humbled me in my pain and sorrow until my pride and arrogance became a distant memory. He let the world destroy me until I had nothing left but Him, and then He built me up again stronger than before in Him. Each time God broke me down and stood me back up; each time He corrected me; each time He answered my prayers; each time I witnessed His great power; each time I shared His Word with a nonbeliever who asked for prayer; the truth of God became apparent and my shield of faith grew in strength. One fed the other. Truth brought about faith, and faith brought about truth.

Covering my feet with the gospel of peace was and is a difficult task. Paul tells us that we must be all things to all people so we might save a few. He wrote, "*To the weak became I as weak, that I might gain the weak: I am made all things to all men that I might by all means save some. And this I do for the gospel's sake, that I might be a partaker thereof with you*" (1 Corinthians 9:22–23).

This is a great struggle for me, but a struggle that I happily undertake. It seems contrary to much of what life has taught me. I've seen it over and over again as the peaceful pacifist is viewed as a pathetic pushover and the strong not only survive, but thrive. Meeting all men where they are so that they might meet you where you are and hear the gospel seems synonymous with loving thy neighbor as thyself: again, very difficult. Unfortunately, the ease with which I love my neighbor is still dependent on who lives next door.

"*The* L*ORD* *is merciful and gracious, slow to anger, and plenteous in mercy*" (Proverbs 103:8) and He expects us to be also. Again, I find myself coming up short. Worse yet, when I do manage to curb my anger, it seems to raise my blood pressure. Walking in the gospel of peace is not for the fainthearted. Hardest of all is the required surrender necessary to pray for your enemies. It often starts with a prayer: "God, give me the strength to do what is right and good. Give me the strength to love and pray for my enemies."

For people to believe what you say when you share the gospel of peace, you must live in the gospel of peace. In Paul's first letter to the Corinthians, Paul tells the Corinthians, ". . . *the Lord ordained that they which preach the gospel should live of the gospel. But I have used none of these things; neither have I written these things, that it should be so done unto me: for it were better for me to die, than that any man should make my glorifying void. For though I preach the gospel, I have nothing to glory of: for necessity is laid upon me; yea, woe is unto me, if I preach not the gospel*" (1 Corinthians 9:14–16)!

Jesus makes it clear that for those of us who are saved and understand Scripture, sharing the good news is expected of us. In the parable of the talents (Matthew 25:14–30), Christ calls the man who was given one talent for safekeeping and multiplied it not, but rather, returned to his lord one talent, a "*wicked and slothful servant.*" Christ then tells us that the servant's lord took the single talent from him and gave it to another servant who had multiplied what he was given.

Although walking in the gospel of peace does require walking the walk and practicing what you preach, it is much more. A good and faithful servant multiples what he is given; it is the fulfillment of the Great Commission. Freely given the salvation of the gospel by grace, it is our Lord's desire that we multiply the harvest by sowing the seeds of our salvation. "*How then shall they call on him in whom they have not believed? And how shall they believe in him of whom they have not heard? And how shall they hear without a preacher? And how shall they preach, except they be sent? As it is written, how beautiful are the feet of them that preach the gospel of peace, and bring glad tidings of good things*" (Romans 10:14–15)!

Fortunately, my publication of *First Vespers* has on occasion given me the opportunity to share my testimony at various churches and book signings, but more importantly, finding the truth of God has given me the courage to speak. One morning on my way into work, I was looking at the floor and thinking about what I needed to accomplish that day when I walked past a female laborer without notice. She stopped me dead in my tracks and said, "Pick up your head and say good morning. The good Lord didn't promise you that you would even have this day."

I then proceeded to tell her about all the things that the good Lord had promised me. We spoke about God many times after that. I gave her a copy of my book and shared many of my poems with her. I saw Vashti or "V," as we affectionately called her, alone one day after lunch and I walked over to ask how she was doing. V told me that God had brought me into her life at just the right time. She had been in grief counseling for the last three years. Her son, who had survived two tours of duty in Iraq, had been shot and killed in Philadelphia, leaving behind eight grandbabies. She told me how the words I had shared with her had helped her through a very tough patch. We both cried a moment and hugged.

Months later, I was led by the Holy Spirit to compose a short, but uplifting poem for V on my drive into work. When I arrived, I quickly wrote the poem down before I forgot it and gave it to V after the morning briefing. That afternoon she came into my office to ask me if I was an angel. She said she thought that I must have been eavesdropping outside the door at her house because the poem was exactly what she needed to hear that day. I replied I was in no way an angel, but that I was apparently a messenger of the Holy Spirit that day.

My feet finally shod with the gospel of peace, I knew full well that a great deal of work and self-development was still required to convert my flip-flops into a pair of worthy boots. Just as with every piece of the armor I had acquired, much work was required. Now fully clothed in the armor of God, I was at last somewhat prepared for dinner with the King and ready for battle *against the rulers of the darkness*

I needed to cleanse myself before entering my Lord's house. I needed to clear my path, shed my baggage, put an end to the traveler, and close the door I had opened so many years ago. It was time for a reckoning.

10

KILLING WOODS

The Reckoning

I had been working at the Salem-Hope Creek Nuclear Station in Lower Alloways Creek, New Jersey, and staying with my sister in Wilmington, Delaware, for several months. There was never going to be a more opportune time for the reckoning. If I was ever going to face my Goliath, it would have to be then. I made plans and covered my tracks so nobody would be looking for me or attempting to contact me for days. I didn't know why, but this was the way it had to be. The words of James, brother of Jesus, played over in my mind: "*As the body without the Spirit is dead, so is faith without works dead*" (James 2:26). It was time to take that leap of faith, to step boldly off the cliff of uncertainty.

Ann, my beautiful wife, planned to spend the weekend with the slot machines and her girlfriend somewhere near Niagara Falls. Ann and Sharon went to play the slots a couple of weekends a year. It was well thought out in advance, and Ann was used to me not calling when she was gambling with Sharon.

My sister believed I was heading off to North Carolina to test drive my motorcycle that had been having some custom work done at the Oak Island Heavy Metal Thunder Shop. I didn't tell her anything different. Pennsylvania was just a hop, skip, and a jump away. I could be in Pennsylvania in twenty minutes and reach my final destination by dark. It was Memorial Day weekend, and I didn't have to be back at work until Tuesday. The stars were aligned. It was then or never.

I knew that if I thought about it long enough, I would surely talk myself out of it, just as I had for the last thirty years. I grabbed a couple bottles of water, a jacket, and some protein bars from my sister's house, filled up the car with gas at the local Wa-Wa station, and headed out.

I made it as far as the Marienville VFW in Marienville, Pennsylvania, in just over six hours using the car's GPS. From that point on, my journey became a little more difficult. I was looking for an intersection in the middle of nowhere, somewhere I had been over thirty years earlier. I had no address to plug into the GPS. I would have to depend on the View Map function of my GPS, an old road atlas that I traveled with, and instinct to guide me.

I drove around the old roads until it was nearly too dark to read the road signs any longer. I pulled up to an intersection, nearly ready to give up. I looked to my left and saw the familiar dip in the woods. I looked to my right, just to confirm, and I saw the clearing of the old logging road. I was right where I wanted to be. I gently pulled my car off the road to my right and drove maybe a hundred and fifty feet over the tall grasses that now covered the old logging road. It was well past sundown by the time I shut the car off and tossed the keys on the dashboard.

I had been planning and preparing for this trip for over thirty years. I figured I had gone over every possible scenario and outcome in my mind. Once I arrived at Blair's Gap, if I was able to find it again, my intent was to walk along the edge of the forest until I felt drawn into the woods at just the right point. That never happened and those thoughts went quickly out the window as soon as I stepped out of the car. I set my sights on a point at the edge of the forest and with no forethought whatsoever, I walked directly into the woods.

The next thing I remember was low-hanging branches poking me in the face and stumbling over fallen trees and rocks. It was now pitch-black in the forest and time seemed to pass slowly. I could have been walking for ten minutes or a half hour when I walked directly into a tree and nearly broke my nose. As I felt my way around the tree, I noticed a break in the canopy just overhead, where a dull patch of moonlight shown on a large, moss-covered, flat rock in the center of what I would estimate to be an eight- to ten-foot clearing in the woods.

It seemed as good a place as any to spend the night. I sat down on the rock and made myself as comfortable as I could. Once I stopped moving, I could hear the sounds of the forest. Every broken twig and owl hoot turned my head. Hearing the life around me, my imagination ran wild, and I began to think about the Pennsylvania black bear population for the first time. I pulled my knees in close to my chest and wrapped my arms tightly around my shins. "What have I gotten myself into," I wondered.

I prepared myself with a prayer. "Holy Father, who art my rock, my rod, and my strength, be with me. Know that what I do is not to test you in anyway; but rather, I fight with my inner demons that I may bring them into submission to your will. Though they are cunning and deceitful, you are stronger. I seek to cast them out forever in your name, my Lord Jesus, Amen."

I settled in for the long haul, the hours till dawn stretching before me, and recited Psalm 23. "*The LORD is my shepherd; I shall not want. He maketh me to lie down in green pastures: he leadeth me beside still waters. He restores my soul: he leadeth me in the paths of righteousness for his name's sake. Yea, though I walk through the valley of the shadow of death, I will fear no evil: for thou art with me; thy rod and thy staff they comfort me. Thou preparest a table before me in the presence of mine enemies: thou anointest my head with oil; my cup runneth over. Surely goodness and mercy shall follow me all the days of my life; and I will dwell in the house of the* Lord *forever.*" And God brought me comfort.

I thought back to when I had seen the finger of God come down and touch the earth. I was working for Pennsylvania Power & Light Company in Allentown, Pennsylvania, living with my sister in Whitehall, Pennsylvania, and commuting home to Medina, New York, every other weekend. It was at a time in my life when I was actively seeking to strengthen my faith and exercise my spiritual growth.

One weekend after visiting my girlfriend in New York, I decided to pray for the entire five- or six-hour drive back to Whitehall, rather than listening to the radio as I usually did. I was a rather young Christian at the time and inexperienced in my prayer life. I had no idea how to pray to God for six hours, so I elected to simply recite the Lord's Prayer for the duration of the trip. I had no idea what I was praying for, perhaps that God would simply tell me He was there and listening. Certainly, God knew my thoughts, would read my heart, and know my intent.

The trip as it turns out was uneventful, or so I thought. As the week went on, I realized I was much more tolerant of people and seldom lost my temper or got upset. The time alone with God had done me good, and I couldn't wait for my next trip home so I could again speak with God and recite the Lord's Prayer.

There was a terrible snowstorm on the weekend I drove back to New York. I began reciting the Lord's Prayer as I pulled out of my sister's driveway. I took 15 North over the Poconos as I did every time I made the trip. By the time I reached the bottom of the mountains, I had driven through every form of wet, slushy, and frozen participation you could possibly imagine.

The pass over the Poconos was a trucking route that was often closed in the winter due to extreme weather conditions. I imagined that 15 North would soon be closed and raced to get to the top of the pass before it was closed so I might simply be told to go down the other side of the mountain as I had intended to do anyway, rather than being forced to turn around and take a three-hour detour. I was driving too fast for the road conditions, and not surprisingly, I did not see another vehicle for my entire drive up the mountain.

I knew I was driving on a layer of freshly fallen snow, but what I didn't know was that the fresh snow was covering an eight-inch thick sheet of ice. As anyone who has ever taken 15 North over the Poconos knows, there is a sheer drop off of several hundred feet with almost no guardrail to the right as you are driving north, and to the left, only mountain.

Nearing the top of the Poconos and still reciting the Lord's Prayer while driving fifty to sixty miles an hour, I lost control of my car and began spinning around in counter-clockwise circles. At first, I saw the mountain to my left, then the ravine on the other side of the road, and then the mountain on my left again. When I saw the ravine a second time, it was clear to me that I was rapidly drifting toward the guardrail and would soon plunge over the edge and down into the ravine.

I stopped saying the Lord's Prayer mid-sentence. I had only time to say one word: "Jesus!" I wasn't swearing or using His name to emphasize my predicament as some would say. I simply called out to Jesus because I knew in that instant I would be seeing Him face-to-face in just a few seconds. I called to Jesus, and He saved me in an instant.

As soon as the Lord's name left my lips, I heard a loud explosion to my left. As my car spun around, I saw the two taillights of a tractor-trailer truck, the first vehicle I had seen on my ascent up the mountain. The explosion I heard was the weight of the empty trailer bouncing up and down on the road in front and to the left of me. A touch of God's finger, the condition of the road, and perhaps a break in the sheet of ice that covered the road caused the rear of the trailer to lift nearly a foot off the road. As it slammed back to earth a second or third time, I saw eight-inch-thick blocks of ice flying to the left and right of the trailer.

My front tires fell into the trench created by the displaced slabs of ice. My spinning abruptly stopped as the car was forced to move forward. As I came to the realization that I was now driving on dry blacktop, I gently applied my brakes and was able to slow down to about thirty miles an hour to keep from hitting the truck that was now directly in front of me.

Just as I got the car back under control, I hit the far end of the trench that once again put me on top of an eight-inch-thick covering of ice. I hit the edge of the ice sheet so hard I thought I might pop both my front tires, but I didn't. I found myself seven or eight feet behind the trailer and going much slower than I had been seconds earlier when I had lost control of the car. I slowly increased the distance between the trailer and my car to thirty or forty feet as I followed the truck down the mountain where the driver pulled in behind a restaurant and I continued my way home. Just as Moses had seen God part the Red Sea with a blast of His nostril, so had I seen the finger of God come down to earth and part the sheet of ice.

Sitting there alone, on a flat rock in the all-encompassing darkness, I relaxed my grip on my legs and took a deep breath. My eyes now somewhat accustomed to the night, I stared deep into the forest to see what, if anything, I could make out in the darkness. Then I heard a voice as clear as fresh spring water from the darkness behind me. "Hey Peckerwood!"

I dropped my legs, pointed my toes, and spun around on my seat with an adrenaline-fueled urgency. Nothing . . . only darkness and the occasional belching of a frog. When I could stand the quiet no longer, I managed to ask in as firm a voice as I could muster, "Is there someone there?" Again, from behind me and in the direction that I had been facing just a moment ago, I heard a short burst of what I would describe as a guttural and uncontrolled smug laughter. Still seated on my large flat stone, I spun around once again and turned to face a sound in the darkness. Then, as if by Divine Providence, it began to rain.

My eyes strained in the darkness as an old man walked toward me and came into focus. He was dressed just as my great-grandfather had seen him, in a full-length slicker and wide-brimmed hat. I knew who he was immediately. There was no question who he was or why he was coming to see me.

Then in the most comforting, old man voice you could imagine, he said, "What brings a young man like you to be so far into the woods so late at night?" I couldn't respond. Continuing, he said, "There are rumors of strange wanderers and seekers meeting up with a mysterious traveler in this part of the woods who grants wishes. I don't put much stock in such things, but then again, if a mysterious time traveler granted my wishes, I might reconsider. I don't suppose you are a seeker are you?"

Then I heard it again, that same guttural, uncontrolled snicker. It seemed to snap me out of a semi-trance, and I finally responded, "I am a seeker of the truth. Surely your gifts must come at a great price for they are offered in secret and given in the darkness of night. The true giver of gifts gives His gifts freely by the light of day and by His divine grace."

The traveler snapped back, "If that were true, then why wouldn't the giver of gifts have already granted you your every wish by his divine grace?"

"He did and He does!" I answered. "Did not John tell us that God hears the prayers of the worshipper? '*Delight thyself also in the Lord; and he shall give thee the desires of thine heart*' (Psalm 37:4). I have the desires of my heart because I delight myself also in the Lord."

The traveler continued, "And what of the familiar spirits you conjured? Shall I call Alfreido and my legion to join us?"

My response was in fear and the words were given to me by God, "*And when they shall say unto you, Seek unto them that have familiar spirits, and unto wizards that peep and that mutter; should not a people seek unto their God, for the living to the dead? To the law and to the testimony: if they speak not according to this word, it is because there is no light in them*" (Isaiah 8:19–20).

And the traveler quoted Scripture back to me. "*Stand now with thine enchantments, and with the multitude of thy sorceries, wherein thou hast labored from thy youth; if so be thou shalt be able to profit, if so be thou mayest prevail. Let now the astrologers, the stargazers, the monthly prognosticators, stand up and save thee from these things that shall come upon thee*" (Isaiah 47:12–13).

The traveler spoke out of context, and again I responded in kind to complete the Scripture. "*Behold, they shall be as stubble: the fire shall burn them; they shall not deliver themselves from the power of the flame: there shall not be a coal to warm at, nor fire to sit before it*" (Isaiah 47:14). Without hesitation, I continued, "At the final reckoning, God will test all the works of man by fire and no such evil work will prevail."

Sometime while I was speaking, I became aware no words were coming out of my mouth. These were my thoughts and not my words. I could easily hear the traveler's words in my head, just as though he were carrying on a conversation with me. I was no longer aware of my surroundings. I felt dizzy and sick to my stomach. I didn't know if it was still raining, if I was standing, or still sitting on my rock. All I saw was the traveler's face looking at me from under the brim of his forward-tipping hat.

At first I saw his face, and then I didn't. Each time I looked to see the detail of his face or the content of his eyes, I could no longer see him. I saw only darkness. He was empty and blended into the night that surrounded me. If I was going to see him, to know where he stood, I would have to follow his silhouette at the periphery of my vision.

My stomach grew tighter as he again placed his words in my mind, saying, "Are not your countless prayers and endless demands from your father for his narcissistic worship the cost of the scraps that fall from his table to the ground for you to pick up like a dog?"

I felt defensive, forgot my uneasiness, and paraphrased my response in anger, "My father brings me rest through His Son who is '*meek and lowly in heart.*' His yoke is easy and His burden is light" (Matthew 11:28–30).

The traveler was quick to fire back, "It sounds like a lot of mumbo-jumbo and empty promises to me. What do you have that was given to you by your father that you can hold in your hand and show me today?"

Again, as if the Almighty had prepared my response, I answered with Scripture, saying, "*According as his divine power hath given unto us all things that pertain unto life and godliness, through the knowledge of him that hath called us to glory and virtue: whereby are given unto us exceeding great and precious promises; that by these ye might be partakers of the divine nature, having escaped the corruption that is in the world through lust*" (2 Peter 1:3–4).

The traveler reasserted himself. "What do you have that I can see or taste, hear, smell, or touch?"

I responded, "Whatever I can taste, hear, smell, or touch is of the flesh." Then I quoted the words of the Apostle Paul. *"The works of the flesh are manifest, which are these; adultery, fornication, uncleanness, lasciviousness, idolatry, witchcraft, hatred, variance, emulations, wrath, strife, seditions, heresies, envying, murders, drunkenness, reveling, and such like: of the which I tell you before . . . they which do such things shall not inherit the kingdom of God"* (Galatians 5:19–21).

The traveler argued, "Surely you cannot group the intentional taking of someone's life in the same category as having consensual sex outside of marriage."

I replied, "It is not I, but God who sees them the same. A sin is a sin and '*God is no respecter of persons*'" (Acts 10:34).

The traveler was relentless. "You are well past your prime and have spent your entire life working with nothing to show for it. Perhaps you are too old to be tempted by my gifts. You may not live long enough to ever enjoy your just rewards, but what about your boys? What of legacy and stock options? Perhaps your boys might enjoy a large cabin bought and paid for . . ." I found myself listening when I should have been arguing.

He continued without missing a beat, ". . . each on a private island with stock options so neither one of them would ever have to work again?" I pictured it in my mind for just a second; it was quickly accompanied with ugliness, greed, and bickering. The traveler must have sensed my thoughts and continued, "Perhaps—"

I cut him off there, "Did not my Lord say, '*For what shall it profit a man, if he shall gain the whole world, and lose his own soul*'" (Mark 8:36)?

The traveler was quick to respond with, "Who are you to condemn the pleasures of the flesh that you yourself partook of and were the champion of many?"

I was taken aback, but held my ground and managed a response. "Who better to discuss the rising of the cake than the retired baker?"

The traveler was unyielding. "Are you telling me your hands are now clean because you no longer stand in the kitchen?"

"No," I responded, "my hands are clean because they have been washed clean by the blood of the one who enforces the law. The jailer can no longer keep the one who the judge has set free." I marveled at how the Lord placed Scripture on the tip of my tongue to wield as the sword of Christ.

The traveler fired back, "If it is not a gift that can be seen or tasted, heard, smelt, or touched, it is not of this world."

"The truth rolls off your lips," I said, "but you cannot hear it. So it is with the love of a mother for her child or the charitable act of one stranger to another; they are of God, not of this world."

The comforting old-man voice disappeared. The traveler now spoke in the tone of an angry and bitter old man. "You self-righteous little prick, do you have any idea of what I can do while your father stands around and watches? I can snap you like the little twig you are or bring you enduring pain that will haunt you your entire life."

I was glad that my first response was not fear; but rather, I spoke with the boldness of Christ. "You wield righteousness around like it is an insult to be feared. Do you not know that righteousness is an honor to be sought?" Again, I swung the sword that is the Word of God against the angel of iniquity. *"Be glad in the LORD, and rejoice, ye righteous: and shout for joy, all ye that are upright in heart"* (Psalm 32:11). And "*The eyes of the* Lord *are upon the righteous, and his ears are upon their cry*" (Psalm 34:15).

The traveler's voice shifted to a soothing monotone. I felt the power of it, as though I was somehow resisting the urge to be hypnotized. He said, "Sit with me and we will talk as friends."

I asked, "What need have I to sit with you? I have been given the most precious stone that is more prized than the darkest ruby and rarer than the most flawless diamond."

The traveler said, "Give me this stone and I will crush it and give you one hundred more."

I answered, "I cannot for this is a stone so heavy that even you would not be able to lift it."

The traveler laughed his annoying laugh and boasted, "This world is mine to do with as I wish. There is no stone too big for me to carry for I can send a legion to retrieve it if need be."

I replied, "It is the precious cornerstone and foundation to Zion that God Himself has laid (Isaiah 28:16). It is the Christ."

Obviously not liking my response, the traveler snapped back, "Who is this Christ and what is it that he has given you that I cannot double?"

My response was the response of the saints. "He has purchased for me today forgiveness with His blood and granted me eternal peace with His marrow."

"I decide what gifts to share, with who, and when," the traveler said.

I spoke as though I were speaking with the tongue of God Almighty, saying, "You were given charge over little and your reign is short!"

The traveler interrupted. "Enough! Enough! Sit with me for a moment."

Again, the words of Scripture rose up within me. "*Ye cannot drink the cup of the Lord, and the cup of devils: Ye cannot be partakers of the Lord's Table, and the table of devils*" (1 Corinthians 10:21). I asked, "Do you not already do the work of your father by picking the weeds from His harvest? Did He not create you and will He not destroy you?"

The traveler conceded. "Perhaps I have nothing for you. Leave me the stone that was your father's and we will part company."

Suddenly, I was aware of flames shooting up around us as the traveler spoke. The flames were two-dimensional, like the flames of an Amish fireplace or a Yule log on television at Christmastime. They put off no heat, and I had no fear of being burned. I thought of Shadrach, Meshach, and Abednego coming out of the furnace of Nebuchadnezzar unscathed, and I said, "You tempt me greatly, Satan, because I know God greatly, but one thing I know for certain is that fighting you with my father's stone is like fighting a grass fire with a handful of straw. It is idolatry, an offense to God, and your strength. I bring no stone with me today. Instead, I come prepared with the Word of God and the knowledge of what I have learned from my father's stone."

Satan promptly replied, "I know Scripture better than you will ever know it. Now tell me, little man, what could you possibly have surmised from your father's stone that I should fear?"

I answered as if the words had been prepared for me. "The stone is only a remnant of slag from the bottom of a glass furnace, and yet, there remain dimples of glass that cast a light at a great distance when in the reflection of the sun. Surly even in the darkest of furnaces, there remains hope through the light of the Son, even the furnace of hell. Did not Christ preach the gospel in hell after His death on the cross? "*Who shall give account to him that is ready to judge the quick and the dead? For this cause was the gospel preached also to them that are dead, that they might be judged according to men in the flesh, but live according to God in the spirit"* (1 Peter 4:5–7). But the end of all things is at hand: be ye therefore sober."

I spoke boldly. "Surely those that have witnessed Christ storming the gates of hell, preaching the gospel for three days, and walking out of the pit unrestrained know that He is the Son of God and He was given power over death. Believing in the Son of God and knowing the price that has already been paid for the forgiveness of sins, do not these same souls now wait for the salvation of the Second Coming when the gates of hell will be swung open? Do they not wait for the final judgment that will set them free? Is there not already a light of hope that shines brightly in the deepest reaches of hell? The jailer can no longer keep those who the judge has set free for they are free indeed. Then having found eternity in Christ, who will seek anything from the one who burns in the lake of fire? The end of your reign approaches as a roaring lion."

I heard the blast of a thunderous explosion as a blinding white light shown around me like a flash of lightning, and I fell to my knees. I felt as though I had been struck in the back of the head with a ball-peen hammer. The traveler spoke no more, and the darkness of the forest slowly gave way to the breaking beams of morning light. I was alone.

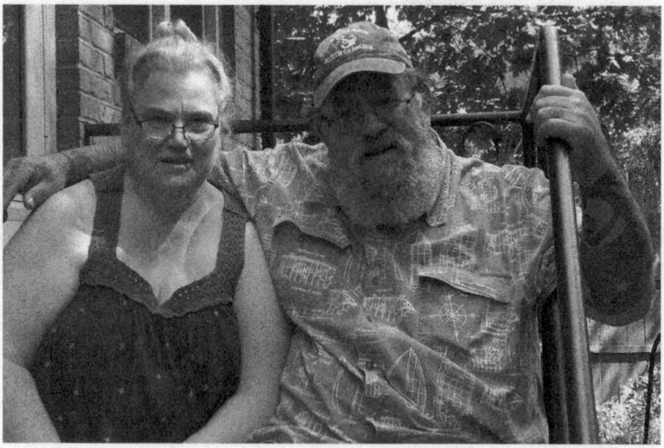

EPILOGUE

For generations (four that have been documented) our family has kept our history and intuitive abilities secret. David and I grew up knowing we could not share with others the inherited curse that followed the men through my father's side of the family, or our intuitive abilities that continue to be passed on to each new generation. Because of this instilled cloak of silence, I was initially very hesitant to support David in this writing endeavor. However, he showed me there is value in sharing his story, the truth of his life.

David's story is a journey of self-discovery and healing. He ties the threads of his life together to form meaning through what he experienced and what he learned from those experiences. I shared a part of his journey, and he kindly included me in the telling of his story.

David was not the first male member of our family to resort to alcohol/drugs to dull the ability to see what was not there and to hear what was not audible. But he is the first to find his way out of the darkness and feel the need to share it with others. I was side by side with him through the childhood years and our unorthodox upbringing, which was the result of our mother's open-mindedness and acceptance of things unseen. It was not her open-mindedness or acceptance that I feel was at fault. I feel it was more the lack of experience, discernment, and knowledge about spiritual matters that left the door wide open for anything and everything to come through and it did. To this day, I will not touch a Ouija board or anything similar.

Growing up, we tried to hide our differences from others. I resorted to being very serious and studious. We were as different as night and day in our approach to life and the pathways we eventually chose. Despite our different approaches, we accomplished the same thing; we distanced ourselves from others and, as a result, no one got close enough to learn our secrets during our formative years. It was a pattern that continued well into our adulthood.

With maturity, we have each found a respect and tolerance for each other's individuality and different chosen pathways. I developed my skills as an energetic healer, light worker, shaman, and teacher/instructor. Both of our pathways, though different, end in the same place, at home with the Divine, with a mission to serve our Creator by helping others find their way home through self-discovery and self-healing. This story is the story of David's truth, and in the telling, part of it is my truth.

Patricia Burdick Briggs
MSN, RN4, CCRN, HTCP, HTCI/1